DANCE WITH THE DEVIL:
A VALLEY FALLS NOVEL

Jason Brannon

This book is a work of fiction. Names, characters, places and incidents are either the product of the author's imagination or are used fictitiously. Any resemblance to actual events or locales or persons, living or dead, is entirely coincidental.

ISBN:

CHAPTER 1

The sound of breaking glass made Solomon Sharpe sit up too quickly on the sofa. He cursed as the pain behind his eyes blossomed like cherry bomb explosions. He pulled his .45 from beneath the dingy green couch cushion and surveyed the room with one half-opened eye, holding the gun out in front of him like a protective ward.

A whiskey bottle lay in pieces beside the coffee table. Poe, the black cat who was also the guardian of Sharpe's humble abode, stared at him with emerald eyes, proclaiming his innocence. Sharpe and the cat maintained an uneasy friendship. At the moment, he didn't believe in the cat's innocence. But the throbbing in his head made it impossible to do more than stare bleary-eyed at the feline and try to remember why he had gotten into this line of work in the first place.

The cat made an attempt at playing nice by walking over to rub against his leg. Sharpe swatted half-heartedly at the animal and received a hiss in return.

The simple act was enough to make colors dance before his eyes. His ribs felt like kindling that had been broken, doused with kerosene, and lit with a match. He gingerly raised his shirt and saw a patchwork of yellow and purple bruises, and the memories of how they'd gotten there came rushing back. His head swam as if filled with wet cement, and the inside of his mouth felt like it had been carpeted in green shag.

He nearly blacked out trying to get to his feet. He sat back down on the couch for a moment, clinging to consciousness and dignity.

At first, he wasn't sure what time it was. It seemed like he had been asleep for hours, but a quick glance at his watch showed that it was only a little after 5:00 in the evening. Solomon sighed. He hadn't even been out for an hour.

"Sweet angel of death, take me now," he groaned as he set his gun on the scuffed coffee table and clutched his head with both hands. The death angel tattoo on his forearm—which he had affectionately named Bram—seemed to mock him, laughing at his predicament. The reaper waved his scythe in jest, amused at Solomon's current situation. Sometimes he liked to have imaginary conversations with the characters inked on his body when he was trying to reason something out or talk something through. It probably wasn't the healthiest way to ponder a problem, but then again, when had he ever done things the way they were supposed to be done?

He had felt like this on far too many occasions to count after a drunken night of celebrating a closed case. But he wasn't hungover, and he hadn't tested the limits of his liver's capacity to process alcohol the night before. It was the goose egg on the back of his head—and not whiskey—that was to blame for the feeling of nausea in his gut. It was the beating he had suffered at the hands of an angry man that accounted for the aching in every extremity of his body.

Normally, running surveillance on a cheating spouse was easy money. Typically, though, that sort of work was predicated on the fact that the cheating spouse didn't know they were being watched.

This time had been different.

This cheating spouse had known…and she had told her lover that they were being spied upon. Incidentally, the man was a mixed martial arts fighter with a specialty in Muay Thai. The rest of the story basically wrote itself from there.

After obtaining some cursory information from his client, the suspecting husband, earlier in the day, Solomon knew that the object of his surveillance normally took lunch around 2 in the afternoon. The husband had found a matchbook from The Hideaway Motel —one of Valley Falls' seediest motels —in the wife's car, which gave Solomon a starting point. The job seemed like a slam dunk.

Solomon had parked his car in the motel parking lot at one o'clock in hopes that the lovebirds would make an appearance today. It was supposed to be quick and easy money.

He had spent an hour camped out in his car, which smelled like week-old burgers, soggy fries, and cigarettes smoked down to the filter. Then, a little after two o'clock, the lovebirds showed up, pawing and grabbing at each other like a couple of randy teenagers. Solomon had taken a few pictures of the pair as they went into their room and then had little to do but sit there as he waited for the lunch hour to end.

He made the mistake of closing his eyes for a few minutes, thinking that he had time to relax while the lovers did their thing. He was planning to take a few more snapshots when the adulterers came back, when out of nowhere the driver's side window of his gold 1998 Buick Century shattered into a million pieces. Apparently, Muay Thai Guy had come out of the motel room while Solomon was resting his eyes. Without warning, Solomon was hauled through the empty window out into the parking lot.

The fact that it was in broad daylight seemed to make no difference to Muay Thai Guy.

From there, the memory was fragmented.

A flurry of fists and kicks delivered by military-style boots. Solomon's camera being hurled against the pavement where it shattered into a million Chinese-made pieces. A few more kicks to the ribs with a few insults and profanities sprinkled in for good measure. Then, darkness.

Although he couldn't be sure, Solomon thought Bram, his death angel tattoo, might have been laughing at him when this last part happened. Bram had a cruel sense of humor and was usually most amused whenever Solomon was getting the crap beaten out of him.

The thing about getting beaten up at The Hideaway Motel is the guarantee that there will be no witnesses. Every occupant is blind, deaf, and dumb. It's one reason why The Hideaway is so popular. Want to score drugs? The Hideaway is your place. Want to buy a handgun that's had the serial number filed off? The Hideaway is your place. Want to step out on your husband? You guessed it. The Hideaway. More illegal activities happened at this roach motel than at any other place in the city.

New cops were usually assigned to The Hideaway because it provided training on the most crimes in the shortest amount of time. It was just that kind of place. The locals knew to avoid it. The criminals knew to frequent it. All the good private investigators in town knew to make a trip there during whatever investigation they were working on because there was a good chance it factored in somehow.

All Solomon knew about The Hideaway was that he never wanted to see it again.

After laying on the pavement for what seemed like an hour (but was probably only a few minutes), Solomon remembered staggering to his feet. The side of his face was swollen and covered in a gooey mixture of blood and sweat. Gravel and bits of glass stuck to his cheek. He tested his teeth with his tongue, and one of them wiggled when it shouldn't have. The inside of his mouth tasted coppery, like he had been sucking on a penny.

Solomon managed to get back into his car and then promptly passed out. When he woke up, it was because a bum was tapping on his windshield, hoping Solomon could spare a dollar. The bum stopped once he got a good look at the man behind the wheel.

Solomon started his car and drove slowly all the way home, doing everything he could to resist passing out again. He made it to the front door of his crackerbox apartment, managed to insert the key into the lock with a hand that shook like someone afflicted with a palsy, and promptly collapsed on a sofa that looked like it had been color-matched with baby puke.

As he ran back through every detail about the case that had resulted in him getting the crap beat out of him—one in a long line of memories he wouldn't mind forgetting—he also thought about the amount of the check he had received as a retainer for the job. It wasn't enough. Not nearly enough. He needed a new line of work.

With a series of groans, and a lot of effort, Solomon Sharpe got up from the sofa and made it to the kitchen table. He found a bottle of aspirin that he had neglected to put away, and he shook three into his hand. The effort was painful enough that he reconsidered and shook a fourth pill out of the bottle for good measure. He popped the white tablets into his mouth, grimacing at the chalky bitterness, and downed the last vestiges of day-old coffee that swirled around in the bottom of his special cup that said, "Sometimes I talk to myself when I need expert advice." The coffee tasted like it had been filtered through a sweat sock, and he winced at the taste. But he managed to get the aspirin down.

Alani, the hula girl tattooed on his other forearm, danced and swayed and smiled at him. "You should take better care of yourself," she said, moving to a rhythm that only she could hear.

"No kidding," Solomon said, thinking he might need to be checked into Saturn Hills Asylum if he kept talking to his tattoos. "Remind me of that next time before I take another case like this. No, wait a minute. What am I saying? I'm asking my tattoo for advice. Forget what I said."

"Remember, what you're doing with me is a trick that you learned in Afghanistan," Alani reminded him. "You were entrenched for three days under heavy fire, and Potter taught you how to do this. It's more of a method of meditation than anything else. You know, I'm not really talking to you, and you aren't really talking to me. It's a way of purging all of those temp files in the memory banks of your mind. Housekeeping is how Potter described it."

"Housekeeping," Solomon muttered. "Sure, that's what this feels like."

"You've solved a lot of cases by housekeeping," Alani reminded him. "Sometimes the answers are there, buried underneath all the details. You just have to do a little cleaning in the corridors of your mind to uncover those answers."

"Is there any method of housekeeping that will fix my busted ribs?"

"I'm afraid not," Alani answered. "This is more of a mental

process than a physical one."

Solomon nodded and gingerly touched his side. He winced and groaned, but he didn't think he had any permanent damage, though he would be sore for a while. Getting beaten up every now and then went with the territory when you decided to be a private investigator in Valley Falls, a strange little town with a penchant for violence and depravity.

Solomon knew he was a mess and decided the thing he needed most was a hot shower. It would be good therapy for aching muscles, would wash all the dirt and blood away, and would hopefully make him feel better.

The shower pressure in his building was virtually nonexistent, but the water heater worked just fine. It took him a couple of minutes to undress because his body moved much slower through aches and pains than it did under normal circumstances. The delay gave the shower time to get steamy.

He took a hard look at himself as he stood in front of the mirror and evaluated what he saw. Salt and pepper hair. Three-day stubble that was mostly black with the occasional patch of white mixed in for good measure. A body that was still in decent shape for a man in his forties. Crows' feet around eyes that had seen more than their fair share of hurt and pain. A mishmash of white scars marking his chest and arms in various places that were the result of bullet wounds, knives, and a few that had been made with the smoldering end of a cigarette during a torture session that one of the local mob bosses referred to as an interrogation.

Yet, despite all of the physical reminders of what he did for a living, everything still worked as it was supposed to. Solomon Sharpe was like a good used car: dinged up in more places than you could count, but still dependable enough to get the job done.

He thought about his father, Alphonse Sharpe, one of the richest and most successful men in all of Valley Falls, and the founder and CEO of Sharpe Enterprises. Quite likely, Alphonse Sharpe was getting ready to have dinner at some Valley Falls hotspot. He would order the most expensive things on the menu of the most exclusive restaurant. He would pay without caring that the bill was more than his son would make in a month, and he would tip generously without even considering that his son was fighting for his life in the Valley Falls underbelly.

Solomon had never wanted anything from his father and had been determined to become successful on his own. Now was one of the first times he truly questioned whether he made the right decision or if there might still be time for the prodigal to come home to open arms and a place at his father's table. He wasn't ready to ask just yet, but he was tired of struggling. Maybe working at Sharpe Enterprises wouldn't be such a bad thing. At the very least, he knew it wouldn't involve getting curb stomped by unseen enemies, and that was important. Sad, how such criteria had come to define what separated the good employment opportunities from the bad.

Clouds of steam had started to gather around him like ghosts of the people who had died in the apartment building. He stepped into the shower and gasped as the hot water poured out over his aching body, sluicing away dirt and caked-on blood and grime. The way the water swirled and spiraled down the drain reminded Solomon of his own life and his current career trajectory. Standing there, a broken man with a broken life in a broken place, Solomon Sharpe leaned his head against the mildewed tile and paused for self-reflection. This wasn't how things were supposed to be. This wasn't how his life should have turned out. Here he was, a reasonably smart guy with a considerable set of skills, bleeding and battered in an apartment that looked like it was made more for vermin than humans.

He needed something bigger, something with a higher profile than a bunch of surveillance cases. He needed a case that would give him a hook with Valley Falls P.D. He needed an important job, a noble job that would justify what he did for a living. He needed a case that would make him feel like he was doing some good in the world. A case like that usually required clients with money, not those needing dirty deeds done dirt cheap.

Solomon stayed in the shower until the hot water ran out, then he carefully dried off and dressed in ratty jeans and a Black Sabbath t-shirt. He passed by the kitchen table on his way to the refrigerator, grabbed the orange juice carton from inside, and took a long, chilled gulp that made his head hurt from the cold and his ribs ache from the effort of swallowing.

Then, he paused, realizing there was something on the kitchen table that he had overlooked.

It was a bright red envelope that had his name on it in a handwritten scrawl.

CHAPTER 2

Unsettled, Solomon retrieved his .45 and searched his apartment, opening every closet door and looking in every conceivable place that someone could hide. He lived alone. No one else had a key to his apartment but Mr. Roper, the building superintendent. And Mr. Roper wasn't one for leaving notes.

Which meant someone had gotten into his apartment while he was out.

Solomon froze when he realized that wasn't quite right either. It had only been twenty minutes or so since he got the aspirin from the kitchen table. The note hadn't been there then. He was certain of it. He would have noticed a bright red envelope with his name on it. He had been out of it, but not *that* out of it.

Someone had been inside his apartment while he had been in the shower. He checked the front door and couldn't find any evidence that it had been forced or tampered with. Which meant the door lock had been picked. He opened the door and examined the doorknob. It was battered, scratched, and beaten up like just about everything else he owned, making it impossible to tell whether or not there were scratch marks made by a set of lock picks. Solomon didn't need to see the evidence, however, to know that he wasn't crazy. Seeing the telltale signs of a break-in would have simply confirmed what he already knew deep in his heart.

The thought made him angry and made him feel vulnerable. Someone had been there in his private space without his knowledge, and although he was now holding a gun, he didn't feel safe. He searched the apartment a second time for good measure. He found nothing other than the envelope.

He looked at the envelope carefully. His name, "Solomon Sharpe," was written in a strong cursive hand in thick looping characters by someone who obviously valued penmanship. A calligraphic flourish had been added underneath his name for effect, but there was nothing on the outside to indicate who the envelope was from.

Carefully, he lifted the unsealed flap of the envelope and pulled out a postcard. On the front of the card was a caricature of a devil like the kind featured in vintage Halloween costumes and on the labels of certain varieties of potted meat. On the back was a simple note written in the same sprawling, elegant hand:

I'm known for my deals, and this one will be of particular interest to you. You will take on a very special case in exchange for the return of your sweet Emily. Something terrible happened at The Hideaway Motel, room 5A. Find out who did it and expose them. No police, and no excuses for your failure. This business involves only the two of us.

The note was signed "The Devil."

If Solomon Sharpe was a balloon, then the note was a pricking needle, instantly deflating him. He collapsed into one of the battered kitchen chairs, reading and re-reading the note. "No," he said. "It can't be…"

But the investigator in him knew that this wasn't a game or a trick of some sort. It was real. Intuitively, he lunged to the scarred cabinet where he kept his liquor and grabbed the first thing he could get his hands on. It was a half-filled bottle of bourbon. He went to take a long swallow of the amber liquid and then stopped, realizing what he was about to do. The bottle and hundreds of others like it were the reason why Emily lived with her mother now and why her mother no longer lived with him.

Solomon spun the cap back on the bottle and stumbled to his bedroom, grabbing his phone off the nightstand. He found Jenny's number in his list of contacts. Although nearly a year had passed since the divorce had been finalized, she was still listed as 'Baby' in his phone. He hit the call button and waited on the phone to connect.

Jenny picked up on the second ring. "Solomon, thank God. I was just about to call you," his ex-wife said, nearly out of breath.

"You were?" Solomon asked. The knot in the pit of his stomach grew tighter. Jenny never called him unless she needed something.

"Wait. Why did you call me?" Jenny asked, a note of panic in her voice.

"Where is Emily?" Solomon asked.

"Please tell me you're joking," Jenny said. "Please tell me she's with you."

"It's not my weekend," Solomon said. "I would never just up and take her. She's supposed to be with you. Why don't you know where she is?"

"I don't know," Jenny said, beginning to cry. "I thought she went over to Marcie's house after school. Marcie hasn't seen her. None of her friends have. I've called them all. Nobody saw her since school let out. I've been driving around the neighborhood looking for her. I was about to call you because I thought maybe there was a small chance she was with you."

"I swear she isn't," Solomon said as he started to feel clammy and sick to his stomach. "Have you tried her cell?"

"Of course I have," Jenny answered with an obvious amount of irritation in her voice. "She didn't pick up. She hasn't answered my texts either. They are showing *delivered* but not *read*. Do you know something about this?"

"No," Solomon lied. "But I will go out and find her."

"Wait a minute, Solomon. You called me and asked where Emily was. There's something you aren't telling me."

"Jenny, I need you to be calm."

"Solomon, talk to me. What do you know?" Jenny asked in a voice that had gone up an octave.

"I'm sure she is fine," Solomon said, digging the hole of deception just a little deeper.

Jenny's voice changed abruptly, becoming cold and hard-edged. "Why did you call me? It can't be a coincidence that you just ring me up out of the blue asking about Emily when she is missing."

Solomon sighed, unsure of what to say exactly. At last, he decided on the truth because it was all he had. "I think someone took her."

"Took her?" Jenny said. "What do you mean? Who? Oh, Solomon. Our baby!"

"I don't know exactly," Solomon admitted. "Someone broke into my apartment and left me a note. They offered me a deal to get Emily back. I have to work a case for them."

"Someone is using our daughter to get to you?" Jenny said.

"What kind of mess have you gotten her into? What have you done?"

"I didn't do anything," Solomon protested. "Promise. This is as much a shock to me as it is to you. I don't know who could be responsible for this."

"That's not good enough for me," Jenny hissed, wavering near that dangerous place between angry and frightened that manifests itself in tears and words spoken through clenched teeth.

"I will get her back," Solomon said. "I know where to start looking."

"I'm calling the police," Jenny said.

"No!" Solomon shouted. "The note said no cops. It's too risky to ignore the instructions. Let me handle this. I'll get her back. I promise."

"You promised lots of things over the years," Jenny said with obvious disdain. "Your word doesn't mean that much to me anymore."

Solomon knew he was wasting precious time and that he had to be very careful with what he said next. The clock was ticking. "I know that I made a lot of mistakes," he offered, trying to seem contrite. "You didn't deserve to be treated the way I treated you. When times got hard, I retreated. I drank. I was so miserable that I was looking for anything to dull the pain."

"Including…her," Jenny said, refusing to speak the name aloud of the woman who had torn their family apart.

"Including her," Solomon admitted. "But the one thing I never did was neglect Emily. Despite all the ways I hurt you, I tried to shelter her. She's always been what keeps me going. I love her more than my own life, and I will do whatever it takes to get her back safely. You have to believe that. Please, let me handle this. You know how much she means to me."

"You hurt her in ways you didn't even realize," Jenny said, her voice crumbling a little. "But I know you've always thought she hung the moon, and the feeling was mutual for her. I shielded her from seeing the worst about you, and it's one thing about the end of our marriage that I'm most proud of. I didn't want her to see her daddy like that, drowning in a bottle of booze, and finding comfort in the arms of another woman."

"I'm so sorry," Solomon said, meaning it. "I'm ashamed of who I was then. But I'm not that person anymore. I'm crawling out of that hole, inch by inch, day by day. I'm not at the bottom of that dark place anymore. Where I'm at now, there are periods of light, and those periods of light are the things that keep me going, that get me through each day. Emily is the source of that light, and I will not lose her."

"I believe that is true," Jenny said. "You're becoming more like the person I used to know. I only wish it hadn't taken so long for you to find your way back to us."

"Then please let me handle this. I'll get our girl back, Jen. Just please don't go to the police."

"You're asking me to do something that's very difficult," Jenny said as she began to cry again.

"I'm good at what I do," Solomon replied. "There are lots of things I can't defend about myself or my behavior, but my work is one area where I excel."

"I know," Jenny said. She paused for a minute as if in deep thought. "Go and get our girl back for us, Solomon," she added at last. "I can't lose her."

"I can't either," Solomon said as a tear slipped from the corner of one eye and traced its way lazily down his cheek. "I'll keep you posted."

"Please do," Jenny said as Solomon hung up.

He raced as fast as his aching body would allow, out to his battered Buick. Thankfully, the car started on the first try. The Hideaway Motel was the last place he wanted to go back to, but he didn't have a choice. He had to get Emily back, and this seemed to be the only way.

"Guess it's time to dance with the devil," Solomon said as he put the car in gear and pulled out of the apartment parking lot with a squeal of his tires. The air blowing through the broken car window felt good on his face. It would be the last simple pleasure he would know for a while.

CHAPTER 3

Pulling into the parking lot of The Hideaway Motel brought back a lot of painful memories. Memories that seemed far older than the last few hours of aching bones and throbbing muscles would suggest. Solomon gave the place a long, hard glance, making sure that Muay Thai Guy wasn't lurking nearby to use him as a punching bag again. Thankfully, all he saw were some junkies, gangbangers, and hookers looking for their next john in the hour before dusk. In other words, business as usual at The Hideaway.

Solomon thought about going to the front desk and asking for a key to room 5A. Frankie DeCarlo, the desk clerk, was a tweaker that would probably let him in for a six-pack or a carton of cigarettes. But Frankie was a loose end that he didn't want right now given that his daughter's life was possibly at stake. He opted for picking the lock to room 5A and taking a peek without authorization instead. If Frankie caught him, he could talk his way out of it.

He had won a set of lockpicks from a retired thief in a poker game a few years back. The training on how to use them had required a bit more effort on his part. The thief had agreed to show him how to develop some skill with the picks in exchange for taking a case that involved finding an old acquaintance who had double-crossed him. In other words, Solomon had to track down the thief that stole from the thief who happened to be his client. The case was long and messy, and in the end, Solomon learned that, in fact, there was no honor among thieves. But his client had been happy with the result and had spent the next two weeks giving him a crash course on the finer points of lock-picking. It was a skill he had utilized many times over the years and was grateful he possessed now.

The relief he felt at being able to access the room without a key quickly turned to abject horror when he opened the door and saw a scene that would have rivaled the killing floor of any slaughterhouse. The walls were covered in scarlet. The sheets were soaked with it. The air was filled with a ripe, pungent stench that made him instantly cover his nose and turn away to keep from throwing up. The handiwork would have made Jack the Ripper sit up and take notice.

Solomon backed out of the room quickly, unwilling to go deeper into the crimson mess. Murders at The Hideaway Motel, while infrequent, were not unheard of. But this was more than that. This wasn't strictly murder. It was something else that was much grander and much more twisted. It was carnage on a scale he had never seen before…and he had served in Afghanistan.

He walked around the courtyard for a moment, taking deep gulps of air to help him think, and to clear the stench of death from his nostrils. He didn't want to go back into that room, into that mess. This shouldn't have been his problem, and yet it was. He sat down on a bench and felt the bulk of his wallet pressing against his hip. Pulling it out, he found a picture of Emily that he had tucked away, and he stared at it for a moment. The picture was taken when she was around five or six. In it, she wore her blonde hair in pigtails. He was holding her in his arms, and she was staring at him with the biggest grin on her face. The sight of it made his heart ache as he thought about how much he missed seeing her every day.

The feeling that followed that one was an overburdening sense of guilt as he was reminded of the things he had done that kept him from seeing her each day. Thankfully, Jenny had gotten over being angry at him for the affair and wanted what was best for Emily, which included a healthy relationship with her father. She hadn't turned Emily against him, and for that, he would be forever grateful. He had promised himself that he would never do anything else to hurt his daughter and would put her first in every decision he made.

The time had come to do just that. He had to go back into that room. He had to solve this case and get her back.

A couple of gangbangers were down at the vending machines getting a snack and filling their ice bucket. Solomon waited until they were gone before getting up from the bench and heading back over to the door which must have been a portal to Hell based on what he had seen behind it. He looked both ways to make sure he wasn't being watched and to verify that this wasn't a setup. Then, abruptly, before he could talk himself out of it, he opened the door, stepped inside, and closed it behind him.

The room was filled with a sickly yellow glow from the bedside lamp. It cast everything in pale, wan light that was reminiscent of sickness and disease. Spatters of blood on the lamp's bare bulb made it difficult to discern details about certain parts of the room. Solomon was careful as he walked around the worst part of the mess and used the tail of his shirt to pull the chain turning the lamp off. Then, he eased back around the bed and turned the overhead on, grateful for the harsh white light from the fluorescents. It allowed him to see better, which was both a bad thing and a good thing.

He could see the body in more detail now. The feminine curves of the body, the painted nails, the lack of an Adam's apple, and the clothing helped him to discern that it was a woman. She was covered in stab wounds that were too numerous to count. He could also see that the woman had a burgundy purse which he hadn't noticed initially because its color blended in so well with all the blood.

After retrieving a hand towel from the bathroom, Solomon used it to open the purse. The driver's license inside identified the woman as Monica Moore. Although it was impossible to tell what Monica looked like from the remains, the picture in the I.D. showed her to have raven hair, brown eyes, and a beautiful smile. The photograph didn't show the extra smile that the killer had added when he slashed her from ear to ear. According to the information on the license, Monica was 31, 5'4", and 115 pounds. Most of those details would have been impossible to ascertain based on the condition of what had been left on the bed.

Despite being petite and beautiful, and looking like she could scarcely hurt a fly, this poor girl had obviously done something to enrage the killer. Solomon had seen a lot of death in his time, and this particular brand of violent, extreme carnage couldn't be attributed to simple opportunity. Passion of some sort was involved here. There was emotion in this act. The room was decorated in spatters of scarlet anger. Only someone out of his mind with fury could do something like this.

In addition to the carnage that had been inflicted on this poor woman, there were additional details that gave Solomon an idea about who was behind this murder. One was the flimsy set of wings that had been affixed to her back, giving her the look of a slaughtered fairy. However, Solomon knew that the idea wasn't to transform Monica into a fairy, but rather an angel. The message written in lipstick on the bathroom mirror confirmed as much. It said: "Isn't it mercy to kill them before they sin so they can become angels? Surely eternity in Heaven is better than forever in Hell."

The name beneath the message was "The Angelmaker."

"God, no," Solomon whispered to himself. The Angelmaker was a serial killer responsible for at least four murders in Valley Falls. The killer's M.O. involved various methods of "transforming" his victims into angels. One of his previous victims had been tarred in black pitch and covered in feathers. One had been forced to wear a halo made of nails. Another had been hanged and positioned in mid-air as if suspended in flight. The fourth had been posed with a harp and strangled with a harp string in a hideous parody. Now, here was the murder of Monica Moore, a fifth victim who had been stabbed unmercifully and given her wings.

Solomon was gobsmacked. He had no connection to any of the Angelmaker's victims, hadn't been asked to consult on any aspect of the investigation, and had none of the resources required to investigate a case like this. How could the Devil expect him to catch a killer that had eluded the police for over a year? He didn't have the pull they did, and he was sorely out of his league. He couldn't even conduct a proper surveillance without getting the crap kicked out of him. What chance did he stand against a cold-blooded murderer like the Angelmaker? He was the wrong person for this. Surely, the Devil knew enough about him to realize that there were far better private investigators for the job. To make matters worse, Emily's life hung in the balance. His success or lack thereof would determine her fate.

Solomon suddenly felt short of breath and knew he was about to slip into a full-blown panic attack. He closed his eyes and put his hands on his knees, taking deep breaths and trying to focus his mind on something besides the situation at hand. After a minute of careful focus, he felt some of the tightness in his chest begin to loosen up, and he was eventually able to stand and breathe deeply. By degrees, the knot in his stomach relaxed a little, and he didn't feel like he was going to be sick.

He knew that Emily needed him right now, and he couldn't let her down. He had theorized that a big case would put him on the map, and this was just that kind of case. Catching a serial murderer that had eluded the police for months would be just the sort of thing to make his name known to the world. He wouldn't have willfully jumped into an investigation like this, but he wasn't being given a choice. Maybe it was best to make the most of the situation, jumpstart his floundering career as a private investigator, and most importantly, save his Emily from the clutches of this person who referred to themselves as the Devil.

It was time to find out just who he really was. It was time to prove himself. It was time to be the father he had always wanted to be to his little girl.

It wasn't an ideal way to catch a break, but as far as Solomon knew, he was the first person at this crime scene. Which meant he would get all of the information before the police. It also meant there might be information here that he could keep the police from obtaining. After all, the Devil had told him not to involve the cops. The easiest way to keep them from catching the killer's trail was to take any evidence he found with him.

Feeling like there might be more to learn from the contents of Monica's purse, Solomon took it to the small table near the air conditioner and dumped its contents out. Truth be told, there really wasn't that much. Some lipstick. A mirror. A brush. A few loose dollars and a handful of change. Nothing strange for the most part. The only thing that stuck out to him was a thick plastic card with the black, embossed image of a cocktail glass set against a glossy gold background. On the flip side of the card, it read only: "The Carbon Underground. V.I.P."

It was a lead, and Solomon was grateful for it since it meant he got to leave this room of nightmares behind. He jammed the card into his pocket, unwilling to leave it for the cops to find. Eager to get back out in the fresh air again, Solomon used the tail of his shirt to open the door.

"Let's see what you've been up to, Monica Moore," he muttered under his breath as he slipped out the door.

CHAPTER 4

Solomon was familiar with The Carbon Underground. It was an exclusive nightclub in Valley Falls, where crime and affluence could be found in abundance. It was a place where a local street drug called Hypnos could be bought without much trouble, exotic liquors like Siren's Wine were kept hidden behind the bar, and all the most edgy bands like Voodoo Mary had been known to play on their rise to superstardom. It was exactly the kind of place he expected to go while investigating this sort of case. Thankfully, he had a hook at The Carbon Underground. Rico, the doorman, had been helpful on more than one occasion, and Solomon hoped that he would be able to provide some information in this instance.

Although it was still an hour until the doors were scheduled to open, the line leading into the club was long and filled with glassy-eyed young people who were all dressed to kill with hopes of elevating their social status by getting inside.

Rico was a big Hispanic guy who looked like he might have been an offensive tackle for the Mafia football team at some point in his life. From the neck down, he was a menace that would make most patrons of the club think twice. The vision from the neck up was completely at odds with that. He had an easy, friendly face that was usually punctuated by a big smile. In fact, Solomon couldn't remember ever seeing Rico upset, even when people were showing their true colors and acting like the overgrown children many of them were. Rico was a nice guy and not the sort that seemed cut out for this line of work. Yet, he was obviously good at what he did. He was a mainstay at The Carbon Underground. The only thing about him that hinted at a darker past was a nasty white scar that snaked from the left side of his shoulder, down his chest, across his abdomen, and over to his right hip.

Solomon was probably one of the only people who knew how Rico had gotten such a nasty scar. A maniac named Nero had tortured Rico for several days in an abandoned warehouse downtown during a reign of terror that paralyzed Valley Falls. Solomon had been instrumental in helping locate Rico. However, he hadn't been successful in stopping Nero. The villain had gone on to kill another five people before going underground. Solomon didn't consider that case to be one of his successes, and he still viewed himself a failure as a private investigator, given that five more people had perished because of his inability to stop Nero. However, Rico had never stopped singing Solomon's praises after that and had been his friend ever since. It was the one positive thing that came out of that case.

Rico saw Solomon coming down the sidewalk, and for the first time Solomon could remember, the doorman didn't have a smile for him. He stepped away from the door for a moment and let another equally bulky guy with a scowl on his face take over.

"Man, what happened to you?" Rico asked. "Decide to change careers and become a punching bag? Trying to look like me? Actually, I wouldn't blame you if I was right about the second part. I am a pretty handsome guy."

Solomon had forgotten about the way he looked after the beating by the Muay Thai bully. "Oh, this?" Solomon said with a dismissive wave of the hand. "Just another day at the office. You know how it is. But if you think my face looks bad, you should see the other guy's fist."

"You look like the south end of a northbound horse, brother," Rico said a bit more seriously. "Hey, did you lose a tooth?"

A look of panic crept over Solomon's features, and he felt around in his mouth to see if there was a gap where one shouldn't have been.

Rico laughed. "Gotcha."

"Jerk," Solomon said. "I thought you were my friend."

"Always, man. Always."

Solomon nodded. "Good, because it's time to prove it. I need a favor. A big one."

"Anything you need. Just name it."

"Are you familiar with a girl named Monica Moore?" Solomon asked.

Rico shrugged his shoulders. "Names aren't something I usually keep up with. I'm more of a face guy."

Solomon thought about it for a moment and then activated a popular social media app on his phone. Within a couple of seconds, he had located a picture of the dead girl's profile. "This is her."

The big man's expression immediately changed. "How do you know her?" he asked.

"How do *you* know her?" Solomon said, repeating Rico's question back to him.

Rico looked around to make sure he wasn't being watched. It was almost comical in a way. There were people everywhere. Most, however, were focused on the door and imagining the kinds of things that went on behind the velvet rope.

"That girl is trouble," Rico said. "If you're trying to get a date with her, I'd advise against it."

Solomon shook his head. "It's nothing like that."

"You're on a case?" Rico asked.

"A big one," Solomon responded, presenting the card he had taken from the crime scene. "Monica Moore was a V.I.P. here. What made her one?"

"She's an escort," Rico said.

Solomon raised an eyebrow. "Really? What made her a V.I.P.? Those kinds of girls are a dime a dozen."

"She knew the right people," was all Rico would say.

"What does that mean? And how do you know about her?"

"I get paid to know things like that," Rico said. "At times there are some very high-profile people here who request access to those sorts of services. Part of my job is pointing them in the right direction."

"You're a regular concierge," Solomon said with a half-hearted laugh.

"I don't enjoy it," Rico said. "I'd much rather be tossing rowdy drunks out on their faces instead. There is one thing..."

"I'm listening," Solomon said.

"Maybe I shouldn't say," Rico said.

"You can trust me," Solomon said. "You know that."

"I know I can, but you wouldn't be here asking about her if something bad hadn't happened. She's dead, isn't she?"

"What makes you say that?"

"It's a logical conclusion."

"Ok, yes, she is dead. The crime scene looks like Jack the Ripper and Jeffrey Dahmer got into a fight over her. The carnage is on a scale I've never seen before."

All of the color drained from Rico's face. "I was afraid

something like this was going to happen."

"Ok," Solomon said. "There are lots of gaps in this story that need to be filled in for me. You're saying just enough to let me know you know something but not enough to really tell me anything. What *can* you tell me about Monica Moore?"

"Not here," Rico said. "Meet me around back in twenty minutes. You follow what I say to the letter. Understood?"

Solomon nodded. He had never heard Rico speak like this before and wasn't quite sure what to make of it.

He went back to his car for the next twenty minutes and thought about all of the decisions that had led him to this point. It was almost dinner time, and the aroma of smoked meats wafted through the broken window, courtesy of a nearby restaurant. Solomon took one deep breath and then doubled-over in pain as his lungs felt like they were filled with broken glass. He would have to get medical attention at some point soon. He had at least one busted rib, maybe more. It was enough to make him think again about what life might have been like if he had gone into the family business. It would have been much less exciting than his current career trajectory, but at least that path would have provided a steady paycheck, benefits, and some stability, unlike the path he had chosen that had none of those things. It would have also provided an entire squadron of his father's best goons at his back at a moment's notice.

As it stood now, he was alone.

Of course, all of those problems could be addressed and dealt with once he got Emily back. Right now, Emily was all that mattered. He had to solve this case quickly. He just hoped that Rico could give him some useful information.

He met Rico at the appointed time at the back of The Carbon Underground. Rico pulled a ring filled with keys from his pocket and selected one that was particularly old and rusted in places. The door he used it on was barely noticeable, and unless you were looking for it specifically, would be easy to overlook. From the look of the room that it led to, this was an entrance where club deliveries were made.

The door swung open easily on well-oiled hinges, and Rico led the way through a storeroom filled with cases of imported beer and top-shelf liquor that were stacked to the ceiling in some places. Abruptly, he turned and went down a hall that led to a set of stairs that descended into the basement. Solomon followed him without question, although he had no idea where they were going.

The basement was mostly used as a storage room. Extra chairs and tables were stacked on a dusty concrete floor. It looked like it had been a while since anyone had been down there.

Rico reached the bottom step and stopped. "Ok, we should be fine here," the big man said.

"Why are we here?" Solomon asked, confused. "I thought you had something to tell me."

Rico nodded. "That's why I brought you down here. We can't take any chances on someone listening in on our conversation. I think we can speak freely here."

"I'm going to level with you," Solomon said. "Someone has kidnapped my daughter. The only way I get her back is to investigate this case. Now, I don't know what I've gotten myself mixed up in, but I can't simply look the other way. Someone has my Emily, and I'm going to get her back. I will overturn whatever stones I have to in order to get at the truth of this case. I will not abandon my daughter. She's just a little girl. And when I find out who abducted her, I have a bullet with their name on it."

Rico's features changed abruptly, shifting from fear to anger in a split second. "Are you serious? Your daughter has been taken? I didn't know. That makes a difference in what I'm about to tell you. I was prepared to bring you down here and lie to you for your own good. But now that I know what's at stake, I can't do that. I'll tell you what I know…even if it puts me in danger. You risked your life for me at one time. The least I can do is to repay the favor."

Solomon nodded. "I appreciate that. Now, what do you know that you aren't telling?"

"How much do you know about the owner of The Carbon Underground?"

Solomon thought about it for a moment. ""The owner is Sidney Reagan, isn't it?"

Rico heard a noise coming from somewhere in the heart of the club and was silent until he was sure the sound was inconsequential. "Yes, that's correct. How much do you know about Ms. Reagan?"

"Not that much. Just that she's a successful businesswoman. I've seen her in the papers a few times. The articles always have something to do with money. She's loaded from what I gather."

"Have you heard any rumors about her?" Rico asked.

Solomon stopped. "O.K., I get that she's your boss and you don't want to say anything that might get you fired. But I feel like a donkey being led around with a carrot. Can't you just come out and tell me what I need to know?"

"The Carbon Underground caters to a very upscale clientele during business hours. After hours, the clientele is even more exclusive."

"Exclusive how?"

"Rich. Powerful. In need of companionship. Ms. Reagan eventually decided it would be smarter from a business perspective if the club could be a one-stop shop. Liquor. Drugs. Women. Keep the business local. Keep all the profits. Monica was an...employee."

Suddenly Solomon understood. "Sidney Reagan is running an escort service out of the club? You can't be serious."

"You said that. Not me." Rico said sheepishly.

"I'm going to share a bit of information with you, and see if this rings any sort of bell for you," Solomon said. "It's important that you tell me what you know...and important that you don't tell anyone that we had this conversation. Lives could be at stake here."

Rico nodded. "I understand. I won't talk to anyone. It would cause trouble for me too if word got out about what I've told you."

"O.K., good. The police don't know that Monica Moore is dead yet. I was led to the scene of her murder by the person who kidnapped Emily. Monica was murdered by the Angelmaker. I take it you're familiar with the name."

Rico's eyes got wide. "Are you serious? Of course I've heard the name. It's been in all of the papers and all over the news."

"I figured as much," Solomon said.

"The police have been searching for that killer for months now."

Solomon nodded quickly, pulling his phone out. "I just thought of something," he said as his fingers darted over the keys. Within seconds, he had pulled up The Valley Falls Observer's website and searched for stories about the victims of the Angelmaker. He showed a photo of one of the victims to Rico. "Did this girl work for Sidney Reagan too?"

Rico studied the photo closely. At last, he nodded slowly.

Solomon showed him another photo. "And this one?"

Rico nodded again.

Solomon repeated the process for the other two victims, and Rico started to look like a bobblehead, nodding his head up and down at the sight of each one.

"So, all of these girls were escorts who worked for Sidney Reagan?"

"All of them," Rico confirmed, glancing over his shoulder to make sure someone hadn't crept up behind him.

Solomon grinned and smacked his open palm with a fist. "No wonder the police couldn't find a connection among any of the victims. They didn't know Sidney Reagan was running a whorehouse out of the back of the club. Now I know what the common thread among the victims is. They were all escorts. Which means it's very likely that the Angelmaker is one of these exclusive clients that you mentioned."

Rico remained silent which caused Solomon to study him carefully. "You knew about the connection, didn't you? You've known all along. You must have."

"I couldn't say anything," Rico said. "These businessmen who come here after hours are very influential and very dangerous. Some of them are also very scary. Their reach is vast, and their power is very broad."

"Who are they?" Solomon asked, demanding more from his friend.

Rico's phone dinged as a text came through. He studied his phone carefully for a moment before focusing on Solomon. Something about what he saw seemed to make him nervous.

"Is everything ok?" Solomon asked him.

Rico studied his phone for a moment more and was silent.

"Rico," Solomon said again.

Rico's phone dinged a second time. He touched the notification on his screen to open the message and read it. His face was a mixture of indecisiveness, fear, and stubborn defiance. Solomon wasn't exactly sure what was going on with his friend, but he knew it had something to do with the two messages he had just received.

Rico's fingers went into gear, typing a reply. Once he was finished, he looked around cautiously. Solomon started to say something, but Rico held his hand up to quiet his friend. He cocked his ear like a dog that hears something no one else can hear. At last, he lowered his hand and looked at his phone again.

Solomon rested his hand on the butt of the gun that was tucked into his waistband. He didn't draw it yet, but he wasn't far from doing so.

"Earth to Rico," Solomon said, waving his hand in front of Rico's eyes, growing uneasy at the reaction the texts had brought out in his friend. Rico didn't answer. Solomon proceeded to pull his gun and held it limply at his side, not sure if there was a threat nearby or not, only grateful for the comfort it provided.

After several seconds of tension, Rico eventually relaxed and rolled his head around on his neck to stretch the muscles. "I'm sorry," he said at last. "Everything is fine."

"You're full of it," Solomon said. "I know you better than

that. You're scared of something. What is it?"

Rico met Solomon's stare, and the look in the bodyguard's eyes was one of panic that was trying hard to be something else. The one and only time Solomon had ever seen this sort of look in Rico's eyes was when he found him right after Nero had finished torturing him. It was a look he had never forgotten.

"I've got something for you," Rico said. "I think it might help you with this case."

Solomon held up his hands. "Look, Rico, I don't want to cause any trouble for you, and I think there are things you aren't telling me. Let me help you."

"Don't worry about me," Rico said.

"I pulled you into this."

"It doesn't matter," Rico protested. "You saved my life once, and now your daughter's life is in jeopardy. I have to help. I owe everything to you, and I won't turn my back on you. I can take care of myself."

"Are you sure?"

Rico didn't answer immediately. Instead, he swallowed hard and then nodded. He looked over his shoulder cautiously again as if someone was in the room with them. Of course, there wasn't anyone else. "I contacted a friend earlier when you told me about Monica Moore. I have a picture from them I just received that I can send you from one of the after-hours parties. Maybe you can find your killer in the photo."

"Does someone know I'm talking to you?" Solomon asked, narrowing his eyes at the phone in Rico's oversized hand. "Is someone watching us?"

"Someone is always watching," Rico said cryptically. "And yes, my friend knows we are talking right now. But we can trust him. He can help us."

"Who is it?"

Rico shook his head. "I can't tell you that. Just trust me. I wouldn't lead you astray…or at least not for a good reason. You know me better than that."

Solomon sighed. "Ok, I guess I don't have much choice in this. Send me the photo."

Rico touched his phone in a few places and then pocketed the device. "Done. You should get it in a second. Just remember that wherever this trail leads you have to follow it to the end."

"What does that mean?" Solomon said, not liking this new, frightened version of Rico one bit.

"Just make sure that you get to the bottom of all this," Rico said. "Expose anyone that needs to be exposed, and show no mercy. The people involved in this don't deserve any."

"I promise, man. You have my word."

"That's all I can ask," Rico said. "You're a good man, Solomon. A true friend."

"Thanks, Rico. I appreciate it. I owe you one."

"Don't thank me yet," the big man responded as a thin rivulet of sweat ran down one cheek. "We may have both just signed our death warrants by getting involved in this."

Solomon waited until the text from Rico showed up before following the bouncer back to the alleyway behind The Carbon Underground. In those brief few minutes they had been inside, it had started to rain. The skies were a deep purple –the color of bruises and nighttime. A heavy, warm drizzle fell from the sky, causing a thin layer of mist to rise up like ghosts sentenced to wander the city streets for eternity.

"Thanks again for your help," Solomon said in the split second before he saw a glint of light from a nearby rooftop that was immediately followed by the blast of a high-caliber gunshot. He didn't have a chance to shout "Get Down!" before Rico's expression turned to sheer terror as he clutched at his throat and made a gurgling noise that sounded a lot like a stopped up drain.

Blood seeped out between his fingers, and he gagged profusely, choking on his own fluids before he dropped like a falling star. Rico was dead almost as soon as he hit the ground. His eyes had a glassy, faraway look in them, and he took one final ragged breath before going limp.

Solomon shouted for someone to call 911, and then he took off running in the direction of the building where the shot had come from.

CHAPTER 5

Solomon didn't really expect to catch the shooter since he wasn't exactly sure where the sniper had been located. He ran in the direction he thought might yield the best results and hoped to see someone fleeing the scene. But lots of people were running, scattering like ants out of a smashed anthill. Women were screaming and fleeing the club area in spandex dresses that left little to the imagination. Their boyfriends were running right alongside them, trying to keep their cool and not appear too frightened. Most of them had reputations to keep up. To Solomon, these people were little more than a distracting afterthought.

Despite the pandemonium, he stood and watched and hoped to see something. In the distance, he heard the wail of sirens, knowing they were meant for his friend, Rico. The thought made his heart heavy. Rico would still be alive if it weren't for him. He had dragged Rico into this-*whatever this was*-and gotten him killed as a result.

He had saved Rico once upon a time. This time he failed. He knew the guilt would be a dark companion that would travel with him for a long time to come. It was more weight that he would have to carry with him as a result of this occupation that he had so stubbornly chosen.

People who worked for Alphonse Sharpe didn't have to contend with these sorts of things. It was yet another reason why he was seen as the black sheep of the family.

After a few minutes – once he was convinced there wasn't anyone of suspicion around - Solomon returned to Rico's body and waited for the police to show up. A thick pool of blood had fanned out around Rico's head, giving him a crimson halo that looked garishly festive and obscene in the harsh glare of the sodium vapor lamps.

The cops arrived quickly, taped off the scene, and took Solomon's statement. He had dealt with both officers before, and they knew who he was. They wouldn't shake him down and try to pin the crime on him. That was above their pay grade anyway. Their job at the moment was to contain and secure the crime scene.

Thinking of the Devil's warning, he made sure not to mention anything about Monica Moore, The Hideaway Motel, or the 'small' fact that his daughter had been kidnapped. Solomon wasn't typically one to follow instructions, but in this case, he was going to do everything the Devil said to the letter. Emily's life depended on it. Instead of telling them why he was really there at The Carbon Underground, Solomon just told them that he had dropped by the club to invite his old friend to a party he was having later in the week. The uniformed officers were skeptical of the excuse he made but did little more than write it down in their notebooks and give him the side-eye. It was a look he was accustomed to.

As he waited for the detective assigned to the case to arrive, he listened to the chatter of those working the homicide and tried hard not to look at Rico's lifeless body lying there on the damp pavement. One of the officers, a guy named Hernandez, reminded his partner, Millicent, that the last time they had gone to two murder scenes in a single night was during the Collector's reign of terror. Solomon remembered the case vividly. He was certain the Collector had nothing to do with this, but just the mention of the name was enough to make him reflect on what a gruesome and bloody little place Valley Falls was. It had more serial killers per capita than any other place in the country and was known for manufacturing sickos in the same way that some towns were known for manufacturing furniture or automobiles.

Solomon couldn't help wondering if Valley Falls might have been built on an ancient Indian burial ground or on the site of some prehistoric pagan ritual. That would have been the reason a movie would have given for all of Valley Falls' trouble. It seemed as good a reason as any for the high strangeness that always occurred inside the city limits of the most famous place in Thornmire county.

Solomon decided he would try to see if he could gain any information from the cops. He approached Hernandez. The guy was usually friendly enough and seemed to enjoy the sound of his own voice judging by the way he talked non-stop.

"You mentioned two murders in the same night," Solomon said. "Obviously, Rico here is one of those. There was another somewhere in town?"

Hernandez studied him carefully for a moment, unsure of whether he should say more. It was uncharacteristic for Hernandez.

Millicent, fortunately, spoke up. "It will be all over the nine o'clock news anyway. The Angelmaker claimed another victim over at The Hideaway."

"That's terrible!" Solomon said, feigning surprise.

Now that the secret was out, Hernandez jumped back in. "From what we hear, the place was painted in blood. A regular slaughterhouse. The victim was a woman just like all the others."

Solomon nodded and chewed on the information. A thought

occurred to him. He had been given specific instructions to leave the police out of things. Yet, he had been led to The Hideaway Motel and gone to the club based on the V.I.P. card he found inside. Now Rico had been murdered in cold blood outside The Carbon Underground. The police weren't likely to connect the two killings, but whoever shot Rico had basically drawn a line between the two locations. Solomon was the common denominator in both locations, although the cops wouldn't know that. They had nothing to connect him to the first crime scene, but he would definitely have to be even more careful going forward. The last thing he needed was to be connected to two seemingly unrelated murders. A good detective would connect those dots and start to build a case against him. That was the last thing he needed right now. It would severely complicate matters and make it that much harder to get Emily back.

The rain had stopped now, and the moon was high overhead, looking down on the whole grisly scene like a rubbernecking pedestrian. Solomon couldn't shake the feeling that he was being watched too. More than anything else, he just wanted to go home, shut his door to this whole mess, and pull the covers up over his eyes so he could hide from it all until it was safe to come out. But Emily didn't have that luxury, and she was the reason he couldn't stop until this whole business was concluded.

A crime scene investigator set up shop, taking photographs, making notes, and writing a thorough account of both the surroundings and the personal details of the victim. Solomon wanted to ask the CSI some questions in hopes of gleaning some information, but he decided against it for the moment. This one was new –a pretty one with dark black hair, brown eyes, and a name badge that read Newton. He hadn't developed any goodwill with her yet. She would likely regard him with suspicion and stonewall him...or think he was trying to flirt and get her phone number (which he made a mental note to try and do once this case was over).

Eventually, a grizzled detective named Wallace Hammett showed up in a slate gray '96 Chevrolet Caprice that looked like it might have been decommissioned by the force after several years of active service as a cruiser and bought at auction. It was the kind of car driven by a man too dedicated to his job and too wrapped up in tradition to try anything modern. It was a detective's car, and you couldn't look at it without thinking 'cop.'

Hammett's eyes were bleary and bloodshot, and it wasn't a stretch to conclude that he had been dragged out of bed for this. No doubt, he was probably mentally evaluating his choice of career in much the same way Solomon had earlier. Detective Hammett's white hair was wild and stood out in wiry sprigs. His clothes were wrinkled. His face was heavily lined. His disposition was less than sunny. He had been on the job for quite a few years now and perpetually wore the look of a cop, even when he wasn't working a case.

Hammett looked at his watch and scowled.

Solomon checked his watch to see what would have prompted such a reaction. It was only a little after 8:30. Not late by any stretch of the imagination. That could only mean one thing: Hammett had a heavy caseload and had likely turned in early for the night after working a long tour. No doubt, the detective wouldn't be thrilled about his most recent assignment. His face testified as much.

Solomon checked his watch again and sighed. It had only

been a few hours since he was at The Hideaway Motel for the first time, taking pictures from his car and thinking about what kind of TV dinner he was going to have for supper. Now, he had a detective with the Valley Falls Police Department giving him the stink eye and pulling out a battered notebook to take his statement about a cold-blooded murder. My, how things had changed.

However, Solomon was grateful that it was Hammett who had been assigned to the case and not that douchebag, Detective Young. He and Hammett were on friendly enough terms, and he was hoping that would come in handy in this case.

"Sharpie," Hammett said, sidling over to him with a sigh. "Like the marker. Right?"

"Just Sharpe," Solomon corrected him. "But close enough."

Hammett nodded and pursed his lips. "Why am I never surprised to find you at my crime scenes?"

"I'm just trying to be like you when I grow up," Solomon said, attempting to inject a little humor into the situation.

Hammett focused on him with a look that was anything but jovial. "I've spent the last twenty-four hours wrapping up a case about a series of murders in Easthaven Forest. Now, I've got a guy with a hole in his neck that's lying in a pool of his own blood. I had just gotten into bed and was nodding off when I got this call. Do you know I was dreaming about Salma Hayek when my phone rang? I'm not in a joking mood here. Let's dispense with the pleasantries. Tell me what you know."

Solomon gave him an abbreviated version of events, leaving out everything about the Monica Moore connection. As far as the Valley Falls police were concerned, that case and this one were completely separate, and Solomon wanted to keep it that way. He played it off like a drive-by, and Hammett seemed to buy it.

"Do you think it was accidental?" Hammett said. "Not accidental as in 'Oops, I accidentally fired my gun and the bullet ripped this guy's throat out,' but accidental as in 'Oops, I was shooting at someone else and hit the wrong guy.'"

Solomon played dumb. "Rico and I have been friends for a while now, but I don't know everything he was involved in. I don't think he had any gang enemies. I don't think he was targeted, but I really don't know. In his line of work, he makes enemies on a nightly basis. It could be anybody."

Hammett chewed on this for a moment and produced a toothpick that he started to gnaw. It was one of the things he did when he was thinking. "Maybe," he conceded at last. "But how many people would kill him for denying them entrance into a nightclub?"

"Have you forgotten what city we live in?" Solomon reminded him. "Valley Falls is known for things that wouldn't happen anywhere else."

"Good point," Hammett said. "Did you happen to see which direction the shooter fired from?"

"I think it came from behind us somewhere," Solomon lied, pointing in the opposite direction.

Hammett grunted and studied the area behind them. At one end of the alley was a group of buildings. Some were divided up as office suites dedicated to tax preparation, graphic design, marketing, accounting, and the like. At the other end –the one Solomon pointed at –was a restaurant called The Chopping Block, a convenience store, and a newsstand.

Hammett pulled a notepad out of his shirt pocket and made a note. "What happened to your face?" Hammett asked. "You look like you've been in a fight recently. Did it have anything to do with this? You were the last person seen with the victim."

Solomon froze. He had forgotten about his appearance again. He knew this didn't look good.

"Rico and I were friends. I would have never done anything like this to him. To be honest with you, I got beat up. I was doing some surveillance for a client and the spouse found out."

"What kind of gun do you carry?"

"A forty-five."

Hammett stepped away for a moment and conferred with the CSI. He came back a bit more focused. "The victim was shot with a .308 so at least you answered that question correctly. Also, we have a witness that places you at eye level with the victim. I think the shooter fired from some place elevated. I don't think you're our guy for this."

"That's what I've been trying to tell you," Solomon said.

"I've heard every word you said," Hammett said. "I've also noticed the things you haven't said."

Solomon's mind raced to interpret that last statement. Hammett was obviously suspicious of him in some way. Or maybe he was fishing, hoping that Solomon would let something slip. Solomon decided to keep quiet for the moment.

"Have you told me everything you know about this?" Hammett asked, focusing on him completely with a look that all mothers who know their children are lying are familiar with.

"Absolutely," Solomon said. "If I hear anything or learn anything, I'll be sure to pass the information along."

"Make sure that you do, Sharpie," Hammett advised. "I don't like being lied to, and I would hate for you to do anything that would ruin the professional relationship we've established over the past couple of years."

"Understood."

"Now, please leave my crime scene," Hammett said.

Solomon didn't waste any time doing as he was instructed. He wanted to be away from Hammett's scrutinizing gaze, which was part of the reason for his haste, but he also needed to find the location where that sniper had set up shop as quickly as possible.

Leaving the crime scene, he headed back in the direction opposite the one he had told Detective Hammett about and went to search for clues about the shooter.

What he didn't realize is that Hammett was behind him, following at a safe distance.

CHAPTER 6

Solomon wasn't sure whether or not Hammett believed his story, but he didn't have time to worry about that at the moment. Despite what he had told the detective, he had a hunch about where the shot came from that killed Rico, and he was determined to focus on that in hopes of learning something about the shooter. If he could find the shooter, it might lead him to Monica Moore's killer, and that was ultimately the key to getting Emily back.

He had seen a glint of light (which he assumed was a reflection from the scope that the sniper used) in the moment just before Rico went down, and he knew the general direction from which the shot had been fired.

The area the shot came from was filled with several office buildings. Solomon was fairly certain that the sniper had set up near a six-story building that was the headquarters for King's Court Technologies. Solomon had done some work for Simon Banks – the CEO of the company – in the past. Based on what he knew about a recent incident at the company, he was pretty sure that the shooter hadn't been parked on top of that particular building.

A while back three of their employees had been murdered on the roof by someone calling themselves The Jester. It had made the news cycle for a couple of weeks before Simon's money and influence made the story go away. In the interest of salvaging his company's reputation, he had taken immediate steps to keep such a thing from happening again which included beefing up security leading up to the roof, and prohibiting anyone from accessing anything above the fifth floor.

Thus, it was highly unlikely that the shooter had fired from the King's Court roof because of the obstacles that would need to be cleared to get up there. But the building beside King's Court Technologies was only one story taller and would have provided the same sort of opportunity. It was also currently unoccupied, making it the perfect place for a sniper to set up shop.

A heavy padlock held a chain together across one of the fire exits. This type of lock was a cinch to crack, and Solomon used his lock picks to gain access. He was forced to use both hands to pull the door open, and he groaned as a fresh wave of pain spread upwards from his abdomen to the center of his chest. It felt like someone was pulling his ribs apart with their bare hands. He took the steps slowly and realized that he wasn't at all equipped for this investigation, even though it would have been fairly easy under normal circumstances.

His lungs felt filled with burning kerosene as he climbed flight after flight of steps to get to the roof of the building.

Thanks, Muay Thai Guy!

The roof was populated by a few birds that took flight when he opened the creaky door. Other than that it was empty. There was no sign that the sniper had been up here. Looking around, there wasn't much to see. Smudges of pigeon excrement here and there. Sticky patches of tar that had been used to seal up leaks in the roof. The occasional roofing tack dropped by some careless contractor. That was about it.

Solomon walked the perimeter of the roof and then

stopped when he saw something that wasn't visible from the door. A small pile of trash had been meticulously left like a memorial shrine dedicated to the sniper's time on the roof. The sniper had been here after all. From the look of things, the shooter had spent a decent amount of time up here, waiting for just the right moment to fire the shot that had ripped through Rico's throat and stolen his life from him. The pile consisted of a variety of unusual things: sunflower seed hulls, two gum wrappers, a couple of cold French fries that the birds hadn't found yet – and a black plastic shopping bag with the white silhouette of a magician printed on the outside and the name 'Arcane Infinity' printed in esoteric script at the bottom. The bag had been spread out flat, and the other trash had been placed on top which weighed it down and kept it from being blown off the roof by a brisk wind.

Solomon studied the bag closely and wondered if someone was toying with him. He picked up the bag carefully, touching only the tiniest part of it as he flipped it over. Two words had been written on the plastic in permanent silver marker: "avra kehdabra."

Surely, this was no simple coincidence. Everything in front of him seemed intentional, planted, left behind specifically with him in mind. It was almost as if the sniper had left these things to give him a lead. This didn't seem to be the work of an amateur, and yet, the tiny hill of junk indicated that the killer wasn't worried that any of it would lead back to him. Furthermore, what kind of killer provided a shopping bag that could potentially provide a clue about where he had been? It was a clue, but it was too convenient. Solomon felt like he was being led around by the nose. But to what end? For what purpose? If someone wanted him to go to Arcane Infinity, why not just tell him that? What would he learn there that would help him with this case?

Arcane Infinity was a place Solomon knew by reputation only. It wasn't because it was a scandalous place or a place where infamous characters committed nefarious deeds. It was a magic shop with connections to the deceased world-famous illusionist, The Amazing Silverstone, and hidden links to a secret society of magicians called The Order of the Left Hand. It wasn't a place that had figured into any of his previous cases. He simply knew it by reputation because part of his job required him to keep his finger on the pulse of the city and know where certain types of information could be found if needed.

He always kept a pair of plastic disposable gloves in his jacket pocket whenever he went out on an investigation, and after putting them on, he bagged up everything he found on top of the roof. Satisfied that he had learned all there was to learn at this particular location, he headed back to his car and thought about his next move.

At this point, he had two choices. He could drive straight to Arcane Infinity as he was certain he was meant to do. Or he could ignore what he had found and pursue a different line of investigation. Even as the thoughts swirled around in his head, he knew there was only one option: to go where the case led even if it felt like a trap. Emily's life was at stake. He needed to get her back, whatever the cost.

Even as he piloted the Buick through the black streets like the ferryman through underworld waters, he knew he could turn right at the intersection up ahead and go in search of more information about Monica Moore's life (who she was, who her connections at the club were, what her reason for going to The Carbon Underground was). Or, he could make a left turn and head toward the magic shop. Solomon knew that the left-hand path signified a turning away from all that was good, and somehow, that choice seemed like the more fitting of the two. He wasn't throwing his morals away, but rather, was running headlong toward a darkness that threatened to swallow him whole if he let it. Yet, at the bottom of that darkness, in the most dismal depths, was sweet Emily. She needed saving, and he was the only man for the job. This was his chance to become something more than he was. This was his chance to find out what he was made of.

Solomon turned left at the intersection and slammed his foot on the accelerator.

As he drove toward Arcane Infinity, Solomon turned on the radio and was surprised to hear the Rolling Stones singing about "Sympathy for the Devil." Thinking that the irony of the song choice was a little too on the nose, he quickly switched the station, settling instead on a hard rock station that was playing the old Metallica song, "Creeping Death." It was a song about the plagues of Egypt, specifically inspired by the movie, "The Ten Commandments," starring Charlton Heston as Moses.

In the movie, the Angel of Death is represented by a green cloud. The cloud, incidentally, represented God's judgment on the people of Egypt after the Pharaoh refused to free the Israelites from captivity. It was a fitting song for a fitting mood. Solomon wanted nothing more than to see whoever this person was who called themselves the Devil get judgment for kidnapping his daughter. Nothing was too severe in his opinion, including a thick cloud of creeping death.

The Buick pulled into the parking lot of the magic shop with a squeal of tires and a belch of noxious smoke. It drove just like Solomon felt: barely able to go, yet somehow still clicking off the miles. Solomon surveyed the outside of the place and thought it to be pretty nondescript. A sign over the door read, "Arcane Infinity, Creating Magic Out of Thin Air." It was as good a slogan as any.

Solomon stepped inside, not knowing what to expect. A cheap bell tinkled as the door swung inward. The store, as it turned out, was both more and less than he expected. It was a mixture of cheap beginner magic tricks displayed on spinner racks, displays of colorful costumes suited for the stage, and counters filled with older, more expensive props that only the most experienced sleight of hand artists would be in the market for. The walls were papered with posters of magicians and illusionists from days gone by and filled with all manner of swords, daggers, and unusual weapons. The Amazing Silverstone, one of Valley Falls' most famous sons and one of the world's most popular magicians, was featured prominently throughout the store alongside others like Thurston, Blackstone, The Great Carter, David Copperfield, Penn and Teller, David Blaine, and many others. A heavy middle-Eastern incense of some sort was burning, giving the place an exotic feel. It was equal parts toy store with items geared for kids who had no interest in learning real sleight of hand, and mystic emporium with a variety of higher-end illusions that would appeal to those who hoped to make a living from their skills. It appealed to both Solomon's inner child which believed that magic was real and the intellectual, adult part of him who enjoyed trying to figure out how the trick was done.

A golden Egyptian sarcophagus stood against one wall. An iron maiden was propped against another. Both of them had to be replicas, although they were each exquisitely crafted. Solomon was studying the spikes inside the iron maiden and marveling at how sharp they were when a movement startled him. He gasped involuntarily.

The hipster that popped up from behind the counter caused Solomon to jump because he hadn't realized that someone was there. It wasn't every day that a man with a waxed handlebar moustache, mutton chop sideburns, and wire-rimmed glasses appeared seemingly out of nowhere. He looked like a throwback to the days of the Industrial Revolution when such a look was the style. The hair on top of his head was slicked back and held into place by some sort of cream that had a faint medicinal smell to it. He wore an expensive white linen shirt that was buttoned all the way up. The cuffs of his shirt were fastened with cufflinks that were made from some sort of purple stones that sparkled and winked in the light of the overhead fluorescents. He had purple suspenders to match that were busy holding up a pair of green corduroy trousers. His neck (and probably most of his torso based on the skin that was revealed) was covered in tattoos featuring a variety of esoteric symbols and magical scenes that made Solomon's ink seem positively boring in comparison.

Solomon studied the man's tattoos briefly and was able to identify a few Egyptian hieroglyphs, an eerie green tentacle that snaked its way around the hipster's neck, an all-seeing eye at the base of his throat that seemed to shift and track Solomon's movements, and a series of Nordic runes that were inked in an icy blue script.

"I'll bet he has the word 'Mom' tattooed on his right bicep," Bram, Solomon's own death angel tattoo, murmured sarcastically from Solomon's forearm. "Probably has a butterfly tramp stamp to boot."

"Shut up, Bram," Solomon muttered. "You're just jealous that his tattoos are more impressive than you are."

"I'm sorry. Were you speaking to me?" the hipster magic shop employee responded.

Solomon didn't answer at first. He wasn't usually the type to be rendered speechless by anyone, but the strange man in front of him had just such an effect.

"Sorry, I was just talking to myself," Solomon said, crossing his arms so as to cover up the death angel on his arm and keep him from speaking up again.

"No problem at all. I do that myself sometimes. What can I do you for?" the man asked in a boisterous voice that would have seemed better suited coming out of a ringmaster's mouth. "My name's Edison."

"I'm Solomon Sharpe. Are you the owner?"

"No, no, heavens, no," Edison said. "He's not here at the moment. Is there something I can help you with?"

Solomon didn't speak at first. It hadn't really occurred to him what he would ask once he got here. He knew any question he might pose would seem unusual at best.

"Are you here for something specific?" Edison asked. "We have all sorts of items suited for all sorts of magicians."

"I'm not a magician," Solomon said. "Truthfully, I'm a private detective."

"I see," Edison said. "What's this about?"

Solomon pulled out the bag and showed it to the man. "Did this come from here?"

Edison pushed his wire-framed glasses down on his nose and peered over them with wide eyes. "Avra kehdabra," he said, spying the word that had been written in silver ink. "It's the old spelling. Not many use that anymore."

"What does it mean?" Solomon asked.

"It's the Aramaic phrase that provides the foundation for the word 'abracadabra.' It's a magic term that means 'I create as I speak.' Where did you get it?"

"I'm pretty sure it was left for me," Solomon said. "I was hoping you could explain why."

"I don't know specifically, but the only people in Valley Falls that use those specific words spelled in that particular way are the magicians and illusionists of The Order of the Left Hand. If one of them left that for you, then it means they are on your side and want to help. It's a signal of sorts."

"Why would I need a magician's help?"

Edison chewed on that question for a moment. "That depends on the problem you're facing, I would imagine," he said at last. "I don't know what you're mixed up in. The fact that a member of The Order of the Left Hand would leave such a message for you indicates that your dilemma is one of considerable magnitude. They take great pains not to expose outsiders to the secrets of The Order. They take even greater pains not to get involved in situations that might cause them to unduly cast The Order of the Left Hand in a negative light."

"What kind of secrets?"

Edison laughed. "If I knew that, they wouldn't be secrets, now would they?"

"This guy really thinks he is cute, doesn't he?" Bram the Death Angel muttered from Solomon's forearm. "Doesn't he know we don't have time to waste?" Solomon covered the ink up with his hand, silencing the tattoo for the second time.

"Ignore Bram," Alani the Dancing Hula Girl said from Solomon's other forearm. "He's just jealous that Edison's tattoos look better than he does. But he's right. We don't have time to spend dancing around the issues here. This situation has gotten more and more serious. We need to find out about The Order of the Left Hand."

Solmon sighed. "You two act like I'm totally incompetent. I'm working on it. Honestly, I'm not sure how I get out of bed by myself everyday without help."

"Sorry," Alani said. "You don't have to be such a grouch with me just because Bram's acting like a petulant child. I'm just trying to keep you on track here."

"You're right," Solomon admitted. "I'm sorry."

"Who are you talking to?" Edison asked. There was a note of caution in his voice. He wasn't exactly sure what to make of Solomon.

"My fault again," Solomon said. "Sometimes I think out loud. It's a bad habit I have. So you aren't a member of this Order of the Left Hand?"

"Not yet," he said. "But I hope to become a member one day. It's not easy, you know? You have to prove yourself worthy to be inducted. Only the greatest masters of sleight of hand are granted access."

"How would I find who left this for me? It's important."

"How important?" Edison asked.

"It's a matter of life and death," Solomon said, thinking of Emily.

Something in Solomon's features must have told a story that his words were incapable of. Edison studied him for a moment before stepping out from behind the counter. He looked up at a bust of Harry Houdini that sat high in one corner of the shop on a glass shelf. Although Solomon couldn't be sure of it, he thought that the eyes of Houdini were watching him.

As if to confirm the theory that he was under surveillance, a voice boomed overhead and said only, "Bring him back, Edison."

Edison nodded, not at all surprised by the voice.

"Follow me," the hipster said as he opened the lid to the Egyptian sarcophagus and typed in a series of numbers on an electronic keypad that was mounted on one inner wall. Immediately, a door at the back of the sarcophagus opened with a whoosh, revealing a doorway which led to another room that was bathed in a brilliant emerald light.

"Now we're getting somewhere," Bram said.

CHAPTER 7

Feeling like he had been dropped in the middle of a National Treasure movie, Solomon cautiously followed Edison into the next room. Immediately, he saw what was responsible for the green glow. The eight-foot-tall statue of Osiris had emeralds for eyes, and a focused light was shining through them for effect, bathing everything in the small room in a warm illumination the shade of oxidized copper.

Osiris, the Egyptian Lord of the Underworld and Judge of the Dead, stood at the head of a boardroom style table, overseeing whatever festivities might take place there. Eight heavy, padded chairs made of exotic woods that had been oiled and meticulously polished were positioned around the table. This was a meeting place of sorts. Yet, only one of the chairs was occupied.

The man who sat at the head of the table, just in front of the statue of Osiris, studied Solomon quizzically. He was younger than Edison by about ten years, but there was something about his eyes that indicated a wisdom and shrewdness which made it clear that he was the one in charge around here. Jet black hair, eyes that matched those of Osiris, and a Van Dyke beard gave him the appearance of a cartoon villain, but the warmth of his smile cut through everything and softened the initial impression he created. There was something familiar about him, although Solomon couldn't quite put his finger on what it was.

"Mr. Sharpe, welcome," the man said as he stood and extended his hand. Solomon extended his own hand and found the man's grip to be stronger than anticipated. The man was dressed in tweed slacks, a smart blue button-down shirt, and a grey vest. He looked more like the librarian for a secret society than the man in charge.

"I am Peter Silverstone."

"Silverstone?" Solomon said. "As in The Amazing Silverstone? Your dad was…"

"That was him," Peter said with some pride.

"I loved watching *The Amazing Silverstone* on television as a kid," Solomon admitted. "It was such a shame when he died. My condolences. I read about the case in the papers."

"Thanks," Peter said. "He was the best. I miss him a lot."

"And now you're following in his footsteps?"

"In a sense," Peter admitted. "I'll never be the master he was. Of course, I know more than a few card tricks and can do some street magic that impresses most people. You couldn't grow up with him as a father and not know how to pull a rabbit out of a hat. But I don't have the hunger for it that he did. He lived and breathed magic. He thrived off the audience and loved seeing their faces light up when he did a particularly impressive trick. I'm a bit more of an introvert."

"Understandable. But you didn't lead me all the way here to talk sleight of hand. Am I right?" Solomon said.

"I didn't lead you here at all," Peter said. "In fact, I'm not sure how you found your way here. Did Rico tell you I was the one who texted him the photo he forwarded to you?"

"That was you he was talking to earlier?" Solomon said.

"It was. I've been to a few of those exclusive parties at The

Carbon Underground and had the photographic evidence to prove it. Rico and I have become friends, and he asked me if I would mind sending one of the photos over. He thought it might help you with whatever you're working on."

"Do you know about Rico?" Solomon asked.

Peter glanced up with a peculiar, puzzled look on his face. "What do you mean?"

"Rico was shot and killed right after you sent him that picture. A sniper got him. An Arcane Infinity bag was left on the rooftop where the sniper set up. That's what led me here."

Peter covered his mouth to stifle the gasp. "Rico's dead?"

Solomon nodded solemnly. "He was my friend too."

Peter ran a hand through his dark hair. "I can't believe this. Did I get him killed with a text?"

"It isn't you who should feel guilty. It's me. I'm the one who involved him in my case. Someone was trying to keep him quiet and stop him from telling me what he knew."

Peter turned to study Solomon for the first time. "What kind of case *are* you investigating?"

Solomon didn't answer immediately. He didn't know Peter and wasn't sure he could trust him. Was it wise to simply tell him everything? For all he knew Peter could be the Angelmaker…or worse, the Devil.

"I'm not sure I should give you the details," Solomon said.

Peter shrugged. "Of course. Of course. You don't know me. I don't know you. I'm sure this isn't the sort of matter you would talk about with a complete stranger."

"A stranger who is part of a secret society," Solomon said with a forced laugh. "I'm kidding, but not really."

"I get it," Peter said, holding his hands up. "Enough said.

I'll have Edison show you out."

"I don't mean any offense," Solomon said. "But this is a delicate situation."

"Understood," Peter said. "Can I have Edison call you a cab?"

"No, I'm good," Solomon said. "My car is outside."

"I want to help if I can," Peter said. "If you think of any way I can assist, please let me know. Rico was a dear friend of mine."

Solomon studied him for a moment. The man seemed genuine, both in his motives and in his grief about Rico. Solomon's gut usually didn't steer him wrong, and his gut told him he could confide in Silverstone. Besides, he had been led here for a specific reason. He couldn't leave without finding out what that reason was.

"Ok, look, maybe it won't hurt to tell you a little about the case. I'll give you the Reader's Digest version. I'm currently investigating a murder that may be part of a series of murders. You've heard of the Angelmaker?"

"Of course," Peter said, raising an eyebrow in surprise. "Who hasn't? You're investigating *that* case?"

Solomon nodded. "A mysterious person who goes by the name the Devil is forcing me to investigate this case in exchange for getting my daughter back. She's been kidnapped. After the Devil provided me with enough information to discover the body at The Hideaway Motel, I ran across a lead that took me to The Carbon Underground. Rico has been a friend of mine for a while now. It just made sense to ask him if he knew anything. I never imagined it would get him killed."

"I don't understand what I have to do with any of this," Peter explained. "I didn't lead you here. I don't have anything to do with the Angelmaker or the Devil."

"Somebody sure did," Solomon said. "I need to figure out why."

"I don't have any idea," Peter said. "But I'll help however I can."

"Someone led me to you just like someone led me to The Hideaway Motel, where the victim was found. Just like someone led me to The Carbon Underground. It all feels like a game of some sort. I'm being driven from place to place. I feel like a pawn in a chess game."

"If what you're saying is true, then I might be in danger as well," Peter theorized.

Solomon hadn't considered this. "I'll be out of your hair soon enough. Just as soon as I figure out why someone wanted me to come here. You obviously have some information I need."

"I haven't the slightest idea why you were led here," Peter said.

"I think you know more than you're letting on about this," Solomon said. "You seem like a guy who knows things, like a guy who has a certain amount of influence."

"And you're basing that on what?"

"Based on the fact that you've attended these high-profile afterhours parties at The Carbon Underground. I'm sure the guest lists for these events are filled with the movers and shakers of Valley Falls. You're obviously on the list. It follows that you must be more than just a magician who is part of some secret magical club."

Peter stiffened and cleared his throat. "I'm afraid I can't help you."

Solomon felt his ears get hot as his blood pressure spiked. He pulled his wallet out and found the picture of Emily he kept there. He slammed the picture on the table. "Look at her!" he shouted.

Peter stared at the picture, but Solomon wasn't convinced

that he had the magician's attention. He pounded the table with his fists. "Look at this little girl!" he yelled. "This is my daughter. She has been kidnapped. If I don't solve this case, I don't know what will happen to her. I've been led to you for a reason. You need to start talking to me and telling me what is really going on here. I will do anything to get Emily back safe and sound. And I do mean anything!"

Peter was frozen into place, startled by Solomon's actions.

At last, he relaxed a bit and sighed. The mask of firm resolve on his face slipped a little to reveal a bit of compromise underneath. "Ok, I'll help you. Your daughter doesn't deserve to be part of this. Let's just say that there is a balance that has to be maintained in a place like this. Valley Falls is a strange town where lots of strange things happen. Someone has to keep things in check. I'm part of that group. That's why we had those after-hours parties. To decide how to maintain order in this place. I was the delegate from The Order of The Left Hand."

"Why you?"

"Because my father did the job before me. I inherited the responsibility...and the right to lead this group."

"You make it sound like a secret cabal runs this city," Solomon said.

"You said that, not me," Peter told him. "Let's just say the heads of all the most powerful organizations attend all of these meetings. The group makes the decisions that keep the cogs turning and the gears moving."

"Sounds like the very definition of a cabal," Solomon said.

"It's a group that acts independently of the Valley Falls city government," Peter said, unwilling to elaborate further.

"You're included in that group?" Solomon said.

"I am," Peter acknowledged. "But that doesn't mean I'm privy to every secret the group has."

"Do you have any idea how these pieces all fit together?" Solomon asked.

"I have a theory," Peter said.

"Let's have it."

"The group of men and women who meet in secret to mold and shape the direction for the city are all used to being in charge. None of them are accustomed to making concessions, to compromise, to meeting in the middle. They are used to having their own way every single time. Not surprisingly, disagreements occur, and there is opposition in the group. There are power struggles. There are those who want to be in charge, to be the leader of the cabal. Some of the meetings are tense…to say the least."

"Which is why Sidney Reagan decided to introduce drugs, booze, and women into the equation," Solomon said. "To mellow things out a bit and make some money."

Peter nodded. "Correct. But nothing has worked to diffuse the situation. There is a power struggle brewing in the group."

"Is the Devil one of the players?" Solomon asked.

Peter shrugged. "It's a solid guess. I've never heard that name assigned to any of the people who are part of the group, but that doesn't mean one of us isn't the Devil."

"I think one of the members of your group is the Angelmaker," Solomon said. "All of the victims are part of Sidney Reagan's harem of girls."

Peter sighed. "I hate to agree with you, but it wouldn't surprise me. There are some very evil people in the group. That's also one of the reasons I'm still a part of it. I want what's best for the city, what's best for the people of Valley Falls. Me and others like me do what we can in our limited ability to balance out the evil, power-driven desires of some of the more corrupt members of the cabal."

"The fact that someone drove me to the Angelmaker's fifth victim – and eventually to you – indicates that they want me to expose the killer's identity."

"Depending on the Angelmaker's identity, that could shift the balance of the group considerably."

"I think all of this might be a coup attempt," Solomon said, thinking on his feet.

"This Devil character is likely the one leading you on this wild goose chase," Peter said. "He's giving you all of the information needed to dispose of the Angelmaker. Then, once his rival is out of the way, he can step in and assume power."

"Any ideas about who the Angelmaker might be?" Solomon asked.

"Have you looked at the picture I texted Rico?" Peter asked. "It's likely that the killer is one of the people in the photo."

Feeling foolish that he hadn't actually studied the picture yet, Solomon whipped his phone out of his pocket. With everything that had been going on during the last couple of hours, he had forgotten all about the texted photo. Yet, he only needed a split second to glance at the image before the sight of a familiar face sucked the wind out of him.

There, amongst all of the secret movers and shakers of Valley Falls, was his father, Alphonse Sharpe.

CHAPTER 8

Stakeouts were Wallace Hammett's least favorite part of the job. He got bored easily, and his mind tended to wander. Also, after several hours of sitting motionless in the driver's seat of his cruiser, his legs usually started to cramp. Then, there was the stakeout food that wreaked havoc on his gut. His doctor had cautioned him about the kind of diet he kept, but it was difficult to eat kale salads and drink protein shakes while on duty. Burgers and fries with the occasional taco and piece of fried chicken were the menu items most days. Of course, he usually did what he could to stave off the negative effects of what he ate. The diet soda cans in the back seat were proof that he wasn't totally ignoring his health.

He was a detective not a yoga instructor. He smoked too much and drank his fair share of whiskey to chase away the memories of every bloody crime scene he had ever investigated. The thought of exercise made him chuckle and run a hand through his salt and pepper hair. "I need a vacation," he muttered to himself as he watched the front of Arcane Infinity. "A stiff drink and a chair on the beach. That would do wonders for my health. All I need is a break from this screwball town and the wackos that live here."

He sighed, wishing that Sharpie would get a move on and do whatever he was planning to do next. Wallace didn't think that the P.I. was a suspect in the bouncer's murder, but he did think that Sharpie knew more than he was letting on. Sharpie had shown him that much when he left the scene of the crime and headed in the direction opposite the one where the sniper had supposedly set up shop.

Having been a detective for as long as he had, Wallace had a gut feeling that the private detective was hiding something, and he was determined to find out what it was. Of course, he had secretly followed Solomon, watched him go up to the top of the empty building next to King's Court Technologies, and tailed him all the way from there to Arcane Infinity where he had been for the last half hour.

Wallace needed to close this case quickly. He had been told to do so by people who were far more powerful than the Chief of Police, and he wasn't foolish enough to ignore the command. This case was the tip of a very big iceberg, and there were players involved who pulled all the strings despite skulking in the shadows. Wallace didn't know the specifics about why this case was so important, but the details weren't important, only the results.

Solomon Sharpe was headed down some very suspect lines of inquiry, and Hammett had been told to stop his progress at all costs. Even if it meant charging Sharpe himself with the murder. Hammett wasn't ready to resort to that because it would be illegal and untrue. Above all else, he still prided himself on his skills as a detective and on his ability to stay on the right side of the law. Besides, he wasn't sure about the motives of the people who were leading him around by the nose.

In the grand scheme of things, he was a small cog in the greater machinery of Valley Falls. But he had been around and played the game long enough to know that things worked much differently in his town than they did in other places. He also knew that self-preservation was an important skill to master, and he had done a fair job at that over the years. The trick here was to close the murder case quickly and lead Solomon Sharpe away from whatever he was chasing. Normally, Wallace Hammett didn't try to please everyone. In most cases, you couldn't. However, in this particular investigation, he didn't have much of a choice. There was only one goal: preserve the identities of the men who secretly ran this town while solving a murder and keeping Solomon Sharpe from getting too close to the truth. Piece of cake.

All Wallace Hammett really wanted to do was go back to dreaming about Salma Hayek.

As he waited, he chewed on a toothpick, trying to understand how a dead bouncer at The Carbon Underground and a magic shop might be connected. There still weren't enough pieces of this puzzle to assemble just yet, but given time, he would get to the bottom of this case. He always did. Tenacity and stubbornness were the key ingredients in his impressively high close rate.

After a few more minutes of staring aimlessly out the window, Hammett began to grow bored. It would have probably been easier to pass the time if he actually broke down and got a smartphone like the rest of the free world. However, he was a creature of habit and his flip phone was all he needed. Calls only, no texts, thank you very much.

His car, likewise, was the automobile equivalent of a flip phone: dependable but old, outdated but still useful. Manual windows. No frills except air conditioning that worked most of the time. And a cassette deck. No CD player for Wallace Hammett. No sirree. A tape already rested in the slot. He pushed it in and listened as Kenny Rogers started singing about the time he met up with the gambler. No matter how many times he heard the song, he couldn't help agreeing with the advice it gave. You gotta know when to hold 'em and know when to fold 'em.

For now, he was going to hold based on the cards in his hand and wait on Solomon Sharpe to make a move. Then, he would evaluate what he did next and devise a strategy. Sometimes, it was simply better to sit back and watch what other people did and then react accordingly.

Wallace didn't know exactly what Sharpie was up to, but he knew it had something to do with the dead bouncer. There had been a wariness in the private investigator's eyes that told a story his lips were unwilling to.

Kenny Rogers had just finished his story about "The Gambler" when Wallace's flip phone made a peculiar sound. He scowled. No matter how many times he told people that he didn't text, they still continued to contact him that way. With an irritated grunt, he flipped the phone open and stared at the text. At first he wasn't sure that he had read it correctly. Then, he read it again and shook his head. It was from David Millington, Valley Falls' Chief of Police.

It read: "Bring Solomon Sharpe in for questioning in relation to the death of Rico Williams. I've been told to erase this."

Wallace and Chief Millington hadn't discussed this case, but he knew that friends in high places had likely leaned on the chief to make this go away quietly. He also knew that he didn't have a lot of choice in the matter. Disregarding a direct order wouldn't do him any favors.

Knowing what he had to do, Detective Wallace Hammett threw the car door open and was heading toward the entrance of Arcane Infinity when Solomon Sharpe came out. The private investigator saw him approach and was more than a little surprised.

"Sharpie," Hammett said. "I need you to come down to the station with me for questioning."

"I'd rather not," Solomon replied.

"It's not a request," Hammett said, hoping the whole thing wasn't about to go south. "We can do this the easy way or the hard way."

"Fine," Solomon said. "Let's just get this over with. I've already told you all I know."

"You can ride with me," Wallace told him as he led the private investigator over to his car. "Get in."

For once, Solomon did as he was told.

CHAPTER 9

Wallace didn't start the car up the minute Solomon got in. The truth of the matter was he didn't know how he wanted to handle this whole thing. He knew what the term 'erase' meant, and he didn't like the way this whole sordid business was heading. As far as he knew, Chief Millington had very strict lines he wasn't willing to cross, and one of those was making a person disappear as a means of eliminating a problem. The text message he had received seemed to indicate differently. If someone had convinced the chief to change his views on things (either through coercion or outright threat), then that meant the stakes in this case had just gotten much, much higher. It also meant certain people in high places would expect him to alter his view on things too. He was willing to look the other way in some cases when nobody got hurt, but it seemed that things were getting a bit too rich for his blood.

Solomon just stared at him, wondering what was about to happen. It was clear he was confused…and a bit on edge.

"Why are you bringing me in?" Solomon asked at last. "I've already told you what I know."

Wallace turned to look at him and chewed on his toothpick a moment before answering. "The truth of the matter is I'm not sure I *am* bringing you in. What you tell me will help me to decide what I'm going to do."

Solomon's face was a mixture of fear and confusion. "I

don't follow you."

"You and I need to level with each other right about now," Wallace said. "I know you lied to me earlier. The shooter took that bouncer out from the direction opposite the one you identified. I followed you, saw you go up to the top of that building, and tailed you here. So, you've already interfered with a police investigation, tampered with a crime scene, and lied to a detective. None of those things surprise me. What does surprise me is why the Chief of Police just told me to bring you in for questioning when he doesn't even know that you're a person of interest in the murder case I'm working. Can you explain that to me? How does he know about you?"

Solomon shifted in his seat. "I can't tell you."

It was clear from the weary look in Hammett's eyes that he had been given this very same answer numerous times over the course of his career and wasn't the least bit interested in hearing it again. "Can't and won't are two different things, Sharpie. Let's try this again."

"I can't," Solomon insisted. "Someone's life is at stake. Someone very close to me. I don't know how, but the person will know if I talk to you."

Hammett looked around warily as if expecting to see someone peering back at them through a set of binoculars. "I'm a detective. I can help you. I just need to know what I'm up against here."

"You don't understand," Solomon said with a note of pleading in his voice.

Wallace shifted the worn toothpick from one side of his mouth to the other. "Here is what I understand. I'm strongly considering letting you out of this car and telling my boss I haven't seen you. As far as I am aware, he doesn't know I've been tailing you and doesn't know that you are in my cruiser at this very minute. I know there is more to all of this than meets the eye, and I need to know that I'm not being played by you for a fool. You can trust me. The fact that I'm about to disobey a direct order should show you that. Anything you tell me, I'll keep to myself as long as it doesn't implicate you in a murder."

"I haven't killed anyone," Solomon said. "I swear to you."

"Then give me something to help convince me."

"Detectives can lie to get suspects to give up information," Solomon reminded him. "How do I know you aren't trying to play me right now and get me to talk?"

"Should I consider you a suspect, Mr. Sharpe?"

"Aren't you?" Solomon asked.

"I'm considering you a person of interest because I know you have information that you are not giving up. You and I have bumped into each other a few times, professionally speaking, and I've always done right by you, haven't I? I didn't bust your chops at the crime scene even though I had every reason to. You're a smart guy. Think about what I'm saying. Just tell me what's going on here. Maybe I can help. Let's pick a different song and different dance. I'm tired of this one."

"I'm not supposed to talk to the cops," Solomon said. "I was warned." It was clear by the wide-eyed look of fear he wore like a Halloween mask that he was genuinely frightened

"Warned by who?"

"I can't say," Solomon insisted.

Wallace narrowed his eyes and nodded. It was clear he understood something at that moment. "Then, let's take a ride. You can trust me."

Solomon knew better than to argue the point and simply shrugged his shoulders as Wallace cranked the cruiser, put it in drive, and pulled out of the parking lot of Arcane Infinity. He drove with purpose and intent, making a series of right and left turns. Solomon wasn't sure where they were going, but he knew for a fact that they were headed away from the police station.

He began to get concerned once they left the city limits of Valley Falls and headed into rural Thornmire County. Hammett took a dirt road that led off the highway and made another series of turns that eventually led them to an open field where empty, damaged shipping containers sat amidst overgrown patches of weeds and scrub. It was the kind of place he expected to find a bootlegging operation or drug deals going down en masse.

"Get out," Hammett said.

Solomon looked at him curiously, then looked at the gun Hammett carried in his shoulder holster.

The detective pulled his service revolver and placed it on the dash of the cruiser as a show of good faith. "I didn't bring you out here to kill you. Follow me so we can talk without fear of being surveilled."

The moment Solomon understood what Hammett was getting at, he hopped out of the passenger's side and headed toward a particularly rust-covered container that had been nearly overtaken by kudzu. One of the doors hung askew, and Solomon walked toward it eagerly.

As far as he could tell, the only witness to this clandestine meeting was the moon, which watched silently and listened to every word, mute about the secrets it overheard.

"Being inside one of these things is like being in an oven," Wallace said. "But we can talk freely inside. This is the place where cell phone signals go to die."

"Sounds good," Solomon said, meaning it. He needed to talk to someone and get this story off his chest.

"I was very careful getting us here," Hammett added in hopes of further boosting Solomon's courage. "We weren't followed. I'm certain of it. I have years of experience spotting a tail. We didn't have one. Scout's honor."

Somewhere off in the distance an owl hooted its encouragement to Solomon to tell what he knew. For a few brief minutes, he was able to unburden himself of his secrets. He told Detective Hammett everything, including the story about the note from the Devil and the fact that his daughter's safe return involved him investigating the case of the Angelmaker's fifth victim. He told Hammett about Rico texting him the photograph of Valley Falls' most important movers and shakers. He recounted his conversation with Peter Silverstone. The only thing he neglected to mention was the fact that his father, Alphonse Sharpe, was clearly shown in the picture he had received in Rico's text. He didn't want to implicate his father in anything until he knew what he was up against.

Hammett didn't say much except to ask a couple of questions for clarification as Solomon told his tale. When Solomon was finished, Hammett was silent. Likely, he was still trying to process all of the information and figure out what it all meant.

"Well," Solomon asked at last. "Aren't you going to weigh in on this?"

"It seems we have mutual friends," Hammett said at last. "I know about the secret group of power brokers who control this city. I normally do what I'm told to do, but this situation is vastly different than what I'm usually instructed to ignore."

"So, what are you going to do?" Solomon asked.

"Do you trust me?" Hammett asked.

"I think I can," Solomon said. "If you wanted to jam me up you could have already done it in a dozen different ways. I think you're one of the good guys. So, the answer is yes. I trust you."

"Ok, good," Hammett said. "Then you and I are going to work together to close this case and get your daughter back."

"If the Devil finds out you're helping me he will kill my daughter," Solomon cautioned.

"That's why he isn't going to find out," Hammett said. "If there's one thing I don't like it's being jerked around, and some of the higher-ups in Valley Falls are getting a little too big for their britches. They think they are above the law. Normally, they are right. But people are dying, and it's time someone paid the price for that. Besides, I can't say I'm being entirely selfless in all of this. Do you know what closing the Angelmaker case would do for my profile in this town? It might be just the thing to get me a book deal and allow me to retire."

"I don't care what your reasons are," Solomon told him. "I just want my daughter back."

"Then let's make that happen."

"How?" Solomon asked.

"First thing's first. You mentioned that Rico texted you a photograph that he received from Peter Silverstone. Yet, we didn't find a phone at the scene of the crime. I found that to be slightly peculiar at the time, but didn't put too much stock in it. Now, I find it to be even more bizarre. I think we should go and have another look in that alleyway and see if we can find this phone. It might have contained some useful information."

"How do we make sure that the Devil doesn't think we're

working together?" Solomon asked.

"Easy," Wallace said with a smile. "You're going to do everything in handcuffs. To anyone watching, it will look like you're my prisoner and I've brought you back to the scene of the crime for further investigation and to corroborate parts of your story. Only you and I will know differently. I'll make sure to cuff your hands in front of you in case you need to use them at some point."

"Ok," Solomon sighed, stepping out from the back of the shipping container, holding his wrists out. "Let's go. I don't have a better solution."

Wallace responded by slapping the cuffs over both wrists. "Sharpie, you have the right to remain silent…" he said with a chuckle. "Oh, and I'm going to take your gun too. An armed man in handcuffs just wouldn't look right."

CHAPTER 10

By now, night had fully laid claim to things. The moon was high overhead, and the city's heart seemed to beat and pulse with the prospect of hidden things. Valley Falls was dark and seedy in places, lit by sodium vapor lamps, and filled with enough shadows to give the creepy city the appropriate level of menace it deserved. Bad things happened in Valley Falls on a regular basis, and it was best that you knew that before stepping foot on the streets at night.

The alleyway where Rico had been shot seemed even more threatening in the moonlight. Shadows pooled in all the places where the streetlights didn't quite reach, and Solomon was thankful that he couldn't see the section of pavement that was stained red with Rico's blood. Rico had been a good friend, and he felt responsible for the man's death even though he hadn't pulled the trigger.

Wallace exited the car and then opened the back door, hauling Solomon out. He was a little rougher with him than he had to be, but he was going to operate under the assumption that someone was watching them. Appearances needed to be kept up, and this needed to look authentic. Solomon still wore the handcuffs and protested loudly about how tight they were on his wrists.

Wallace scanned the alleyway, searching for any place that someone might be lying in wait for them. A stray black cat darted into the shadows when it saw them coming. They could hear the thudding beat of dance music pulsing from inside The Carbon Underground. Apparently, the cold-blooded murder of one of her own wasn't enough to make Sidney Reagan shut down the club.

"Ok, wise guy," Wallace said. "I need you to walk me through this one more time. Tell me what happened, and be thorough."

"I've already told you all I know," Solomon said.

"Tell it again," Wallace said firmly. "And don't leave anything out."

"Rico and I were talking. I saw the glint of light that must have been a reflection off the sniper's scope. I heard a sharp pop that must have been the sound of the shot. The next thing I knew, Rico was clutching at his throat and blood was spilling out through his fingers. He dropped like a rock."

"We didn't recover Rico's cell phone. Did you take it?" Wallace asked, still speaking in an unnaturally loud voice so anyone who might be spying on them could hear.

"I didn't take anything," Solomon said. "I ran toward the spot where I thought the sniper had fired from. I wanted to try and catch whoever killed Rico."

Hammett nodded. "Then, let's look around and see if maybe the phone is still here somewhere."

Both men got down on their hands and knees. The pavement was damp, but neither acted like they were affected by that. The alley was full of trash cans and dumpsters, and the stench of garbage was cloying.

They focused their search in the area around the back of The Carbon Underground. The remnants of a vagrant's box-house filled up a section along the back wall of the club. It was filled with old newspapers, torn cardboard, a few pieces of plastic sheeting, and some clothes. A moldy newspaper showed a headline that read: "The Angelmaker Claims Victim Four."

But they found no phone among the junk.

The trash cans didn't turn up any promising leads either. Then, Solomon had an idea. "I have Rico's phone number. Why don't I just call his phone and see if it rings?"

Hammett stood up and placed both hands on the small of his back, stretching. "Why didn't I think of that? Do it."

Solomon held his hands up to show the cuffs. "Not the easiest thing to fish a phone out of my pocket with these on."

Hammett nodded and stepped in close. He reached into Solomon's front pocket and pulled his phone out. He leaned in and whispered in a voice that was low and urgent. "If we find Rico's phone, I want you to hit me over the head, take the phone, and make a run for it. Don't argue with me. I'm not going to arrest you, but I also can't do my job if I'm having to spend every moment making it look like I have you in custody. Making it look like you've escaped is the only way for us to split up and get to the bottom of this case. It will bring some heat down on you temporarily. Me too probably. But it's the only way."

Solomon heard every word but gave no indication that he did. Instead, he spoke up, protesting loudly. "Can you please get your hand out of my pocket, Detective? Just because you arrested me doesn't mean we're dating now."

Hammett stepped back, scowling. "Stop being a wise guy and make the call," he said, pushing the phone into Solomon's hands.

Solomon nodded and used his thumb to unlock the phone. Then, he found Rico in his list of contacts and hit the call button. The phone rang immediately, lighting up and vibrating under a nearby dumpster. When Rico was shot and fell to the pavement, the phone must have been knocked out of his hands and slid beneath the trash receptacle.

Wallace turned his back on Solomon and approached the dumpster. Solomon waited until the detective crouched over to fish the phone out before clasping both hands together and clubbing him in the back of the head. He pulled back right before hitting Hammett, so as not to seriously injure him, and the detective played his part masterfully, falling into the dumpster and then slumping over in a pantomime of unconsciousness. To anyone who might have been watching, it should have looked like he got the jump on the detective and made a getaway.

Not waiting to see if they were being monitored, Solomon rushed over to Wallace and fished out the detective's handcuff keys which he used to promptly remove his restraints. Then, he grabbed the cell phone from beneath the dumpster and shoved it into his pocket.

He studied Hammett for a moment, uncertain if the detective was actually knocked out or not. He knew he hadn't hit him hard, and this was probably just an act on the detective's part. Still, he felt a little guilty, but he had to move.

He raced out of the alleyway and wasted no time hailing a taxi.

Within less than a minute, a cab driver pulled against the curb. Solomon threw the door open and scrambled in. The cabbie looked over his shoulder and said, "Where you headed?"

"Arcane Infinity," Solomon said. "I left my car there."

The cabbie nodded and pulled away from the curb. "You got it," he said.

CHAPTER 11

The ride to Arcane Infinity was uneventful, and yet, so much happened in the ten minutes it took to go from The Carbon Underground to the magic shop. The first thing Solomon did when he was certain the taxi was headed in the right direction was to check Rico's phone that he had recovered from under the dumpster. The doorman was the trusting kind and hadn't bothered to put a lock code on his screen, so Solomon was able to go to the text app instantly.

The last message Rico had received before getting shot was the photo from Peter Silverstone that likely contained the identities of both the Angelmaker and the Devil. The text he received before that one, however, was the one that got Solomon's attention. It was from someone named Serafino.

The message from that number was short and to the point: "Walk away from this now, and nothing happens. If you talk, you will die. Don't test me."

Solomon thought about Rico's behavior when he asked about Monica Moore, and how something very close to fear had passed across the burly man's face as he received a message of some sort. This must have been what spooked him. Serafino had threatened Rico, and Rico had ignored the threat. He paid for that decision with his life. Solomon scrolled downward on the phone, hoping Rico had communicated previously with Serafino, and that he might learn more by perusing more texts. But there was only the single message sent from Serafino to Rico.

With a heavy heart, Solomon had to admit that Rico knew more than he told. Rico had wanted to help with the case out of a sense of obligation to Solomon, and that loyalty had gotten him shot. But Rico hadn't told everything he knew. In all likelihood, Rico had told him as much as he thought he could get away with and still stay alive. But his gamble hadn't paid off, and now Rico was resting in a morgue locker.

Solomon wasn't sure who this Serafino character was. It wasn't a name he had heard before, and he was familiar with the names of most of the major players in town…or at least the players that were out in the open. Obviously, Valley Falls had a secret group of puppeteers, and Serafino must have been one of them. This was just the break in the case he needed. Most importantly, this was a lead that could possibly help him get Emily back safe and sound.

Before Solomon could think better of the decision and change his mind, he used Rico's phone to call Serafino. The man who answered the phone spoke with a slight Italian accent that was suave, completely relaxed, and carried just a note of menace beneath the cheerfulness.

"Since I had Rico killed, I know this can't be him. So, this must be Mr. Sharpe, Private Eye Extraordinaire. Very pleased to make your acquaintance. I've been a fan of yours for quite some time now. Escaping from Detective Hammett as you did shows an impressive level of skill on your part. It seems you may be a worthy player in this game after all. And yes, in case you are wondering, I have been watching you. I began as soon as I realized you were investigating my extracurricular activities."

"Serafino," Solomon said, trying his best to remain calm.

"I'm happy to finally speak to you. It sounds like this introduction has been a long time in the making. Obviously, you've known about me, but I'm only just now learning about you. I apologize. I normally try to be more prepared."

"Think nothing of it," Serafino said, sounding like the world's most sophisticated shark – refined and reserved despite the bloodlust. "But enough with the pleasantries. Let's get down to business. How can I be of assistance? Surely there is a reason why you called me besides to chit-chat."

"Why did you kill Rico?"

"He knew too much," Serafino answered plainly. "I have spent far too long amassing power in this town for a lowly doorman at a nightclub to bring everything crashing down around me."

"He must have known quite a bit."

"Enough. He worked a lot of private events for us. He knew how all of those girls were connected to Sidney Reagan and her little ring of escorts. A good detective could take that information and narrow down who was responsible for what happened to them. Sometimes it's better to be safe than sorry."

"Oh, I think you will still be sorry in the end. I'll make sure of that."

At this, Serafino laughed. "Perhaps. But perhaps not. I've been in the game for a long time. You don't get to be king without learning a thing or two about self-preservation."

"Let's talk about 'the game' as you refer to it. What is it exactly?"

"It's a contest of wills and of strength to see who can grab the most power in this town and wield it the most skillfully."

"Does this contest sometimes involve killing young girls?"

"Not really," Serafino replied. "Those activities are regarded more as recreation. When you reach the level of the game that I've reached, you look for new things to stimulate the senses, because all of the old vices just start to seem ordinary after a while. I've become numb to the pleasures provided by alcohol, drugs, and sex. Which means I need something different every now and again."

"Is your real name Serafino?"

Serafino laughed again. This time the laugh was a little huskier and a bit raspy. Serafino smoked on occasion from the sound of it. "I've gone to considerable effort to preserve my identity, and you want me to simply tell you who I am. You've got guts. I'll give you that."

"So Serafino isn't your real name?"

"Serafino is the Italian word for seraphim. Are you familiar with seraphim, Mr. Sharpe? Seraphim are regarded as the most powerful angels in God's hierarchy. They are known as fiery beings who are mighty and fierce. Obviously, I know I'm not as mighty as God in our fair little town. But I wield considerable influence and command the allegiance of a certain group of men who can make the world bend to their whims on occasion. And, of course, sometimes I help young beautiful women find their wings as angels when I usher them into the afterlife."

"The police have been looking for you for a while now, Angelmaker," Solomon said, hoping the fear he felt didn't come through in his voice. "You should turn yourself over to them. It would make things so much easier."

This time Serafino's laugh was louder and more boisterous. "You're too much, my friend. I know there are people within the organization who think I've taken too many risks with my extracurricular activities. They are afraid my angel making will jeopardize everything we've worked so hard for. I know this small contingent of people want me replaced. But I've taken some safeguards against all of that."

"So, you aren't going to turn yourself in?" Solomon sighed. "I guess that means I will have to track you down and drop you at Detective Hammett's feet myself. It's the only way to clear my name now."

"Right you are, my boy," Serafino agreed. "At this very moment, an all-points bulletin has been issued for your arrest. Every cop in Valley Falls will be looking for you because you escaped Detective Hammett's custody. Things don't look good for you right now. Somehow, I suspect you won't get close to me."

"We will see," Solomon said. "I'll be in touch."

"Oh, one more thing before I go," Serafino said. "I'm sure you've been turning one little mystery over and over in your brain. No doubt, you've wondered why in the world a clue leading to Arcane Infinity would have been left behind by the man I hired to kill Rico. The truth is, it was left there on my strict instruction. I needed you to visit the magic shop. I needed to connect you to the magic shop before my hitman did the second thing I told him to do and went after his next targets. I think you'll find that your situation has become somewhat more complicated since you were here earlier, and what a stroke of luck that your car was left in the parking lot. Even I couldn't have planned this any better. I've taken another one of my enemies off the board, and I've made it impossible for you to investigate me. Honestly, Mr. Sharpe, the police now suspect you of multiple homicides. First, Rico, and now this."

Serafino hung up the phone just as the taxi turned onto the street where Arcane Infinity was located. Solomon had no idea what was going on at the magic shop, but the parking lot was a swirling sea of police lights.

CHAPTER 12

"Change of plans," Solomon told the cabbie quickly. "Take me two blocks over and drop me off."

Immediately suspicious, the cabbie cocked an eyebrow at the request but didn't argue. The driver didn't want any trouble, and the quickest way to avoid that was to get rid of the fare in the backseat. He gunned the engine, eager to travel the two blocks as quickly as possible.

Solomon threw a wad of cash at the taxi driver and jumped out of the backseat once the vehicle slowed down. He had been dropped off in front of a parking garage, and he walked into the shadow-filled depths of the first level to collect his thoughts for a moment without being seen by any police that might be driving by.

This situation was not good. He didn't know what had happened at Arcane Infinity yet, but he knew that he was being framed for it. Serafino was two steps ahead of him and doing whatever it took to bring the heat down on Solomon. The cops were sure to discover his car sitting in the parking lot and make the connection. Given that they already thought he had knocked out Detective Hammett in the alleyway, fled police custody, and were likely considering him as a suspect in Rico's murder, they were sure to tie whatever crime had been committed at the magic shop to him too. Solomon knew Serafino had just placed him under the microscope in the eyes of the Valley Falls Police Department, making it that much more difficult to out him as the Angelmaker killer.

The only advantage he had at this point –and it was a small one to be sure –was having Detective Hammett in his corner. If Solomon somehow got arrested, Hammett could always vouch for him and tell everyone that the attack in the alleyway was staged. Or at least he could do that so long as he was still alive to tell the tale. Solomon knew he was being paranoid, but he also knew that the paranoia was well-founded. He had no doubt that Serafino had the clout to have Hammett killed too if the situation warranted it. Hammett was the only thing standing between him and a life sentence right now.

Serafino seemed to be holding all the cards here.

No, he definitely couldn't take any chances on getting apprehended. He had to be careful and make no mistakes. He wasn't used to being that good. This, however, was a different set of circumstances, and perfection was required.

After taking several deep breaths to calm himself, Solomon headed toward Arcane Infinity to see what was going on. He knew from the number of units that had arrived on scene that something terrible had happened. He just wasn't sure what.

He took great pains to keep to the shadows, moving into darkness at the first sign of a vehicle approaching from either direction. Thankfully, several of the streetlamps were broken, which made the task of walking undetected a little easier.

He made it to the corner opposite the lot where Arcane Infinity was located. A couple of cars were parked on the street, and he tried the doors on both. He breathed a sigh of relief when one of the doors opened and he was able to slip inside a rust bucket Cadillac with one of those dancing hula girls on the dash.

The sight of the bobblehead was enough to awaken the tattooed hula girl on his arm who had a word of advice for him. "Think back to Afghanistan, when you had to stay still for hours at a time. Your life depended on it then. Your life depends on it now."

"Thanks for the reminder," Solomon said.

Not one to be outdone, Bram, the death angel on his other forearm, also needed to make an appearance. In a way, the two were like the angel and the devil on his shoulder. One usually gave good, sensible advice. The other seemed to only laugh at his misery.

Bram didn't disappoint. "You're the only guy in the world that can be doing exactly the right things and get exactly the wrong outcome," Bram said with a chuckle. "You didn't do anything to get mixed up with the wrong crowd, and yet, now you're mixed up with the wrong crowd."

"Shut up, Bram," Solomon said as he slumped down in the seat and slid over to the passenger's side to avoid detection.

Carefully, he eased up like a crocodile rising out of dismal waters, until his eyes had cleared the door enough to peek out the side window at the scene in the Arcane Infinity parking lot. There were four patrol cars with flashing lights, and two ambulances that had decided to get in on the act by turning their flashers on as well.

Solomon's eyes grew wide as he watched two paramedics roll a gurney out. He couldn't see who was on the gurney because the person was fully covered by a black body bag. If the cops thought he had killed Rico and whoever the person was on the gurney, a manhunt was likely the next step in this process. He imagined his face being plastered across every news station, on social media, in newspapers. Everyone would be on the lookout for him, and someone would eventually see him. He couldn't simply run off into the sunset, not with Emily's life still at stake.

His life had just gone from bad to worse.

Was the dead person on the gurney Edison or Peter Silverstone? Solomon got an answer to that question a moment later when a second gurney was rolled out carrying Peter Silverstone. Peter was still alive and moving, but he seemed to be covered in blood. Which meant that Edison was likely the body in the black bag. If Peter really was one of the secret movers and shakers of Valley Falls, then it was probable that Serafino had given specific instructions not to kill him. Edison, however, had been fair game. Solomon noticed bullet holes in the brick facade of the building, and saw that the plate glass window at the front of the store had shattered as well. Serafino's sniper, no doubt, was to blame.

Solomon's options were limited. Getting his car back was out. No doubt, officers would be stationed nearby in hopes that he would return for it. Of course, that's exactly what he had done, but he hadn't been spotted yet so it would be easy to correct that mistake. Getting Detective Hammett's help was out of the question too since he was still operating to keep up the deception they had created together. In order to close this case, Solomon needed to find out Serafino's true identity, and there was only one lead left that he hadn't explored because he was afraid of what sort of truth it would lead to. Yet, now, he had no choice but to do his job as an investigator and follow the lead, regardless of where it took him.

With a sigh and a deflated sense of defeat, Solomon eased his way out of the broken-down Cadillac and headed out in the direction leading away from Arcane Infinity.

He was going to the one place he never thought he would return to.

He headed home.

CHAPTER 13

Solomon knew his father wouldn't be in the penthouse suite of his high-rise at this time of night. Rather, he would be tucked safely away at home in his leather-bound study, drinking copious amounts of brandy that cost more than Solomon made in a month, poring over some old volume about the finer points of sailing or the stock market crash of '29. He was a creature of habit in that way.

Alphonse Sharpe's company was in the business of hedge-fund management. As captain, he steered this particular ship with an expert's eye and reflexes. Sharpe Enterprises was one of the largest fund managers in the country, and Alphonse was known for his keen sense of instinct when it came to growing the accounts of his clients and earning profits for the company.

Although Solomon had never suspected his father of anything more nefarious than being a prick and an overbearing father whose approval was impossible to gain, the more he thought about it, the more certain he became that his father was somehow mixed up in all of this. If there was one thing that motivated Alphonse Sharpe more than money, it was power. Being part of a group of power-hungry puppet masters sounded like the perfect gig for him. The fact that he was featured in a photograph with this group made it seem likely that he had a secret part of his life that Solomon never knew about.

The Sharpe compound was surrounded by high fences,

monitored by cameras, and patrolled by sentries who made regular rounds to ensure no one snuck onto the grounds. Having lived there for the majority of his life, Solomon knew the security system's weakness and remembered the one place on the back side of the perimeter where anyone so inclined could slip through a break in the fence that was covered by a section of hedge. Because the damage to the fence was covered by foliage, no one had discovered it, and there had been no need to look for a breach since no intruder had successfully made it past the Sharpe security team.

Solomon slipped through the fence undetected and then checked his watch, waiting for the proper time to approach the house. Hoping his old hiding spot hadn't been found by anyone, he lifted up a pile of carefully placed rocks behind the hedge and was happy to see a small yellow waterproof box waiting for him like an old friend. He had stashed this here before leaving his father's house for the last time, grateful it had gone undiscovered.

After retrieving what was inside, he prepared to follow through with the rest of his plan. Like clockwork, the guard made his rounds and headed toward the eastern portion of the property, allowing Solomon to sprint to the side door.

Alphonse Sharpe had begged Solomon on numerous occasions to join the family business and move back into the family compound. Because of that, he hadn't bothered to change any of the locks, ensuring that the key Solomon possessed still fit everything - should he ever change his mind about his choice of careers. This was the one time Solomon was grateful his father hadn't given up on him. He wasn't sure what sort of psychological implications were wrapped up in that notion, but he didn't have time to mentally unpack it all at the moment. He needed to speak with his father.

He let himself in without incident. Most of the house was dark, but he knew it like he knew the back of his hand. He made his way through the darkness with the skill of a cat burglar and was halfway up the stairs when he heard a familiar laugh coming from his father's study - the sound of a young girl's laughter.

A girl he knew very well…

It was a sound that made his heart stop and a flurry of thoughts and emotions race through him.

Throwing caution to the wind, Solomon raced up the stairs and flung the door wide to his father's study. He was shocked and overcome with emotion at the sight of Emily sitting across the table from her grandfather. He resisted the urge to rush over and hug her close to him, until he knew exactly what was going on. The two of them were playing chess. Emily was laughing at the overexaggerated scowl on Alphonse Sharpe's face that came from being beaten by someone only a fraction of his age.

"Checkmate," she said with confidence as she moved her knight into place.

"You've beaten me again," Alphonse Sharpe said, looking up in time to see Solomon at the door.

"Daddy!" Emily said, surprised. "What are you doing here?"

"What are *you* doing here?" Solomon said, repeating the question.

"Granddad asked if I wanted to spend a couple of days with him. He said that he would let you and mom know. I would have texted you myself, but I had an accident with my phone. One of his goons accidentally knocked it out of my hand and into the swimming pool. He's getting me a new phone though. A better one. Isn't that right, Granddad?"

Alphonse smiled, showing far too many teeth. "That's right, my darling. I'll get you the best phone money can buy. Nothing is too good for my Emily. Would you mind giving your father and I a moment?"

"Sure, Granddad," Emily said as she gathered up the chess set. "I'll be in my room. It's way past my bedtime anyway. Mom would freak out if she knew I was up this late. I think I'll just say good night."

"That's my girl," Alphonse said as his granddaughter gave him a quick kiss on the cheek.

When she moved to give Solomon a kiss on the cheek as well, he found himself overcome with a host of emotions as he wrapped both arms around her. Relief flooded through him, and the tension of the past twenty-four hours melted away. His little girl was safe. She had been the entire time. The relief was soon replaced with fury at being played by his own father, but he didn't let that show immediately. Instead, he told Emily that he loved her and watched her head toward the stairs.

For his part, Alphonse was all smiles as Emily went up the stairs. It was a crocodile's smile, too full of teeth and underlying malice. The smile vanished as soon as she did because that's when Solomon made his move and allowed his anger to overtake him. Furious at being played for a fool, Solomon hauled the old man out of his seat and pushed him against a wall of books that were more expensive than anything he owned. A few of them fell to the floor.

"I have been scared to death that my little girl was being harmed, and you've had her the entire time!" Solomon hissed through clenched teeth. "If you weren't my father, I would destroy you!"

Alphonse Sharpe wasn't a man used to being bullied. Despite his age and slender build, he was still quite strong, and faster than he looked. Before Solomon could block the blow, Alphonse had punched him in the kidneys, forcing his son to release his grip. The old man followed with a quick succession of punches to the breadbasket. Solomon dropped like a rock and curled up into the fetal position as Alphonse Sharpe began to kick him unmercifully.

Normally the picture of poise and elegance, Alphonse looked like a demon possessed as he worked his son over. His hair, usually slicked back, stuck out in all directions, and his eyes were lit with fires of madness.

"You. Will. Know. Your. Place. In. My. House. Boy." Alphonse said, punctuating each word with a kick to the ribs. "Nobody comes at me like that. Nobody!"

The old man, winded from both the attack and the exertion, gasped for breath after he was done kicking his son.

It was the only opportunity Solomon needed.

Solomon staggered to his feet after the last kick and raised the gun he had retrieved from the waterproof box. "Step back!" he groaned. Hammett had taken his gun earlier, and he was thankful he had possessed enough foresight to stash another in a place no one would ever think to look.

Alphonse's eyes went wide at the sight of the gun. "Take it easy with that, Solomon!" the old man said. "I lost control of myself for a moment. I've been through a lot lately."

"You've been through a lot lately? Are you kidding me right now? I've spent the past twenty-four hours getting the crap kicked out of me, worrying myself sick at the thought of harm coming to Emily, staying on the run because I'm now the prime suspect in two murders. And then I find out that my own father is mixed up in something so corrupt that he had to kidnap his own granddaughter to use as leverage. You deal with all of that and then talk to me about going through a lot."

The sheer flood of emotions after getting wailed on by the old man caused his head to throb in several places. Unsteady on his feet, he never took his eyes off Alphonse.

"There are things you don't know," Alphonse said.

"I'm starting to figure that out," Solomon responded.

His legs wobbled like pipe cleaners. He was certain he had at least one broken rib courtesy of Muay Thai Guy. Now, he was certain he had at least a couple more courtesy of his own father. Strange blurry shapes danced in front of his eyes, and he felt like he might be sick at any minute. But he couldn't pass out. Not now.

He wiped his mouth with the back of his hand and wasn't surprised to see a streak of blood. He winced as another cough ripped its way out of him, causing him to expel a spatter of blood that marred Alphonse's ornate white chair with crimson.

"You need medical attention," Alphonse said, holding his hands up to show that he no longer meant Solomon any harm. "Let me summon Bertram to help you."

"Stay away from me," Solomon said. "I will shoot you."

"Yes, I think you will," Alphonse said, realizing that he had severely underestimated his son. "But I guess I deserve that."

"You're the Devil," Solomon said. "You're using me to get your rival out of the way."

Alphonse shrugged his shoulders. "I've been called many things."

Solomon cocked the hammer on the gun. Immediately, Alphonse realized that Solomon was fully prepared to kill him on the spot. "The games end now," Solomon said. "You left that card for me on my kitchen table. You're the one calling yourself the Devil. You're the one that told me to investigate that murder at The Hideaway."

The old man nodded and sighed. "It's as you say it is," he admitted. "But there are complexities..."

"Explain yourself," Solomon said, doing everything he could to keep the hand steady that was holding the gun.

"I needed someone with a considerable level of skill," Alphonse said, choosing his words carefully. "You were the first person that came to mind. This needed to be a family matter. I didn't have anyone else I could turn to."

The statement floored Solomon. His father had never approved of what he did for a living. He felt it was beneath anyone with the Sharpe name to slink around in the shadows, digging up dirt for money. He had always viewed private investigators with disdain, and yet, for the first time, he had acknowledged that Solomon was good at what he did. It was enough to make Solomon hesitate, but only slightly.

"Who is Serafino?" Solomon asked. "I am going to close this case, but only because the man murders innocent girls. Not because I want to help you."

"I'm not familiar with that name," Alphonse said.

"I'm not even sure if that's his real name," Solomon admitted. "I think he's the Angelmaker."

"I don't know who he is," Alphonse admitted. "That's why I needed you. There are people in this town who are much higher up on the food chain than me. They know who the Angelmaker is. I have spent considerable resources trying to determine his true identity and have always come up short. The stakes are higher now, however, and that meant enlisting your assistance."

"Couldn't you have just asked for my help? I've been worried sick about Emily. Jenny has been worried sick about Emily. And the whole time you've had her here playing chess?"

Alphonse held his hands up slowly to show he meant no further harm. "I know you hate me…or at the very least resent me for not being what a father should be to a son. Asking you for a favor was a non-starter. Besides, there are…complexities…with this situation. You don't just think the power brokers of Valley Falls are going to let a private eye waltz in and dismantle the entire system by exposing their leader as a homicidal maniac, do you? This situation needs to be finessed."

"You keep saying there are complexities. What does that mean exactly?"

"It means that even a man like me has weaknesses that his enemies can use for leverage."

Solomon pulled Rico's phone out of his pocket and pulled up the picture he had been sent. "Is it possible that Serafino is one of these men?"

Alphonse studied the picture carefully then shook his head. "No, none of them have the clout to be Serafino. They're all power brokers, but none of them wield more authority than me. And I'm not on Serafino's level. Where did you get this?"

"What difference does it make?"

"It makes a considerable amount of difference," Alphonse said. "If someone is documenting our little meetings, then it could spell trouble for all of us."

"The person I got it from is trustworthy and it seems they are actually one of the good guys trying to use their authority to help people."

"Those are exactly the kind of people you should be worried about," Alphonse said. "Nobody in our group would be classified as one of the good guys. Me included."

"What does mom think about all of this?" Solomon asked. "Surely she's not ok with you being involved with these sorts of people."

At the mention of his wife, Alphonse Sharpe visibly crumbled. Looking as if he was on the verge of tears, he covered his face with both hands. Solomon had been prepared for just about anything but this.

"There is something you aren't telling me," Solomon said. "What is it?"

"Put the gun down first," Alphonse said. "I give my word to you that I won't attack you. I shouldn't have done that. I'm sorry. I lost myself for a few moments. There is much at stake here. You've been stressed out for the past twenty-four hours. I've felt the burden of worry for the last forty-eight."

"Where is mom?" Solomon asked, slowly lowering his gun. "Explain what you mean."

"Come, come," Alphonse said, motioning for Solomon to follow him. Solomon dropped the gun and kept it at his side. But he wouldn't put it away, not until he knew he wasn't going to be forced to use it.

Alphonse walked the length of the room and approached a painting that depicted the Fourth Circle of Hell as described by Dante. Solomon had always been puzzled as to why his father wanted such a grim portrait in his study. The painting was dedicated to the notion of greed, and it showed the souls of the damned divided into two groups - hoarders and spenders - who were pushing large stones with their chests. The stones symbolized the souls' selfish drive to amass fortunes in life. It was a hideous image.

Solomon instantly understood the significance of the painting when Alphonse swung the portrait on a hinge, revealing a wall safe that Solomon had never known existed.

Solomon cocked an eyebrow quizzically. Alphonse smiled tiredly. "There are plenty of things in this house you don't know about," he said. "What I'm about to show you is one of them."

Solomon wasn't sure what he expected Alphonse Sharpe to pull out of the safe, but the one thing he hadn't anticipated was a red envelope just like the one he'd found on his kitchen table. The name "Alphonse" was written on the outside.

"You better sit down," Alphonse said as he pulled out the card that was within. He handed it to Solomon, and Solomon accepted it carefully, certain that he didn't want to see what it said.

He read it anyway and froze as the implications of the words sank in:

Dear Alphonse, we have spent decades building our own personal Kingdom in Valley Falls. Now, there are some who seek to seize power and think they are as mighty as I am. You, like the Devil himself, are among those who toy with the idea of greatness, and I know the idea of being exalted like me has tempted you more than once. Yet, rather than cast you out of my inner circle, I will give you one last chance at redemption. I have your sweet Elise in a safe place and vow not to hurt a hair on her head if you expose the evil Angelmaker for what he truly is. He draws too much attention to us with his bloody habits. Use any and all means necessary to excise this cancer, except the police. You know our ways and understand the meaning of secrecy. No one must know what you are up to.

The note was simply signed, "Milton."

CHAPTER 14

Solomon's head swam after reading the note. "Someone kidnapped mom and wrote you a note demanding that you expose the Angelmaker. Then, you passed the buck and did the same thing to me?"

"Milton doesn't like to get his hands dirty," Alphonse said. "But I have no doubt he will kill your mother if we don't get this matter resolved. I may be ruthless in some respects, but believe me when I say that I would never do any harm to Emily. I just wanted to inspire a sense of urgency. That was the easiest way I could think of. I simply stole a page out of Milton's play-book and made it my own. Solomon, I need your help. Your mother needs your help. We have to expose the Angelmaker for who he truly is."

Solomon had never seen his father this close to begging before. Alphonse Sharpe was cold, reptilian, and heartless in so many ways, yet, he loved Elise Sharpe and would be a hollow shell of a man without her. They were partners in crime, peas in a pod, birds of a feather. She was the closest thing to a moral compass that he had, and her presence in his life was likely the only thing that kept him from reaching the same level of sinister deviance as the Angelmaker.

Solomon briefly felt shame for thinking such a thing, but then remembered the way his father had unashamedly worked him over only a few minutes ago and knew that he wasn't wrong about his assessment of the old man.

"Who is Milton?" Solomon asked.

"Honestly, I don't know," Alphonse replied. "He takes his name from John Milton, who wrote Paradise Lost. He considers himself only a step away from God and acts as if he single-handedly controls everything that happens in Valley Falls. Everything he says is steeped in Biblical allegory and symbolism. He refers to me as the Devil, which is why I adopted the name when contacting you."

"And he has mom? You're certain of it."

Alphonse nodded solemnly. "He does. She went shopping two days ago and never came home. Just so you don't think I'm going to try and pull a fast one, I'm about to reach into my pocket and retrieve my phone. I have something else to show you that will back up my story."

"Do it," Solomon said.

His father did exactly as he had said he was going to do and pulled out his phone. With a couple of quick swipes and keystrokes, he pulled up a video. Even before Alphonse hit play, Solomon knew the sight of what he was about to see was going to make him sick.

The video, which had no audio, showed Elise Sharpe bound to a chair and gagged. Her silver hair was mussed, and her makeup was smudged. But she didn't look like a victim. Instead, she looked like a survivor who was trying to figure out how to turn the tables on her abductor. She should have been terrified of what was going to happen to her, but that wasn't the way she was built. Her eyes held a defiant glare, and the look on her face was one of righteous anger, not fear. She was furious at being held this way. Despite the circumstances, Solomon couldn't help being proud of his mother for not letting her captor see her crumble.

The video only lasted ten seconds or so, but it was enough to convince Solomon that his father was telling the truth about his mother's abduction.

"I received this a couple of days ago along with the card. Obviously, I have been taking this seriously."

"Ok, so you're telling the truth," Solomon conceded. "Do you think Milton will make good on his threat?"

"Milton's reputation precedes him. He's known for his wrath. Failure is one thing sure to invoke it. If I don't do as he's instructed me to do, he will kill your mother. There is no doubt in my mind."

"So let me get this straight? All he wants is for you to put a stop to the Angelmaker's exploits because they draw too much attention to your little cabal?"

"That's about the size of it," Alphonse said.

"Why you?" Solomon said. "Out of all the movers and shakers, why are you the one he chose?"

Alphonse studied the ground for a moment before speaking. "I have a reputation when it comes to taking care of problems. I do what needs to be done no matter the cost."

"You're a fixer," Solomon said.

"Of sorts," Alphonse agreed.

"And how is it that you don't know which member of the inner circle is running around killing women?"

"As I told you before, there is a sort of hierarchy involved. I'm not as high up as I would like to be."

"You're a footsoldier," Solomon said, taking a small amount of satisfaction in the fact that his father actually answered to someone else.

"I'm more of a general," Alphonse said. "But there are still a few in power who are above me."

"This little club is one of the rare places where you aren't in charge. I'll bet that's taken some getting used to."

"It's true, and because of that, your mother is currently in danger. She's my weakness. Milton knows that. Just as Emily is yours. I know that as well."

"We have to get Mom back," Solomon said. "I'll help. I would have helped without all the cloak and dagger."

"Milton said no one was to know," Alphonse said. "We have to make sure it still appears that way."

"Can you keep Emily safe?" Solomon asked.

"She's safe here. I won't let her out of my sight." Alphonse said. "Now that I know the score, I will spare no expense to keep her guarded. But you can't tell Jenny about any of this. Not yet. The entire charade would fall apart. She can't know you've found Emily yet."

Solomon chewed on that for a moment. It seemed like a terrible thing to let Jenny continue to worry herself sick when all the while Emily was safe and sound at her grandfather's house. But he knew that what his father said was true. They couldn't tip their hand. Not yet anyway.

"Fair enough," Solomon said at last. "I know Emily's safe so that will have to be enough for now. Is there anything about Serafino you can tell me? Any detail, no matter how small, could be useful. I know you aren't familiar with the name, but surely you have some sort of information that I can work off of."

Alphonse considered this for a moment. "The only thing that I've heard whispered between members of the group is that the Angelmaker has ties to Saturn Hills Asylum in some way."

"In what way?"

Alphonse shook his head. "I have no idea. That's what you would need to find out."

"I've spoken to him on the phone," Solomon said. "His accent sounded Italian or Mediterranean in origin."

"That doesn't ring any bells for me," Alphonse said. "Saturn Hills is your lead. Follow it."

"Fair enough. I guess I need to do some digging at Saturn Hills Asylum," Solomon said, rubbing at his temples to lessen the throbbing in his head.

"That's the next step, but I can't let you leave before we get you patched up. Let me summon Bertram. You need every advantage you can get, and you won't be nearly as effective if you're all busted up."

Solomon considered the sense in what his father was saying and finally nodded. "Call him. I feel like I'm dying here."

Alphonse nodded and went to an intercom system that was mounted by the door of the study. After pushing a button, a groggy-sounding Englishman eventually answered. "Yes sir, how can I be of assistance?"

"Bring the medical kit. My son needs to be patched up."

"Right away, sir," Bertram said. "I'll be down momentarily."

Within minutes, a burly British man with a handlebar moustache showed up in his pajamas and bathrobe. He was carrying a doctor's bag. The next thirty minutes were spent with Alphonse Sharpe's personal physician wrapping Solomon's ribs, administering antiseptic cream to all of the injuries he had sustained over the past twenty-four hours, stitching up two nasty cuts that Solomon had received during his run in with Muay Thai Guy, and administering a handful of painkillers and antibiotics.

"It's not perfect, Master Solomon. But it's better than nothing," Bertram said once he was finished. "I would hate to see what the other fellow looks like. I'm sure he got the shorter end of the stick as it were."

"Thanks, Bertram," Solomon said. "I do feel somewhat better. I owe you one."

"You will need to get those ribs looked at soon," Bertram cautioned him as he headed back upstairs to his sleeping quarters.

"No doubt," Solomon said, casting a furtive glance at his father who refused to make eye contact. "I got worked over pretty good."

Before Solomon could say more to make his father feel even more guilt about losing control earlier, Alphonse went back to the safe and pulled out a packet filled with cash and a burner phone. "This will help you stay off the grid. Lots of people are looking for you. Use it however you see fit."

"Thanks," Solomon said. "It's time to finish this."

"You'd better hurry," Alphonse said. "Your mother's life depends on it."

Solomon nodded and headed toward the door.

"Solomon, there's one more thing," Alphonse said in a voice that was a slight bit unsteady.

Solomon stopped and looked at his father. "Yes?"

"I'm sorry," Alphonse said. "For everything. The fight that drove you to leave home. The way I've treated you over the years. The things I did to you tonight. I haven't been a good father to you. It's something I regret on a regular basis. My actions tonight were born out of panic. I'm so afraid of losing your mother, and the tension of the past two days came out in ways I will never forgive myself for.

"My actions for the other 99.9% of your life had nothing to do with the fate of your mother. I have no excuse for any of that. If we manage to make it through all of this, maybe you will give me a chance to make things right. I'm not proud of the man I am, the man I've become. Standing here in this moment, I realize that every choice I've made leading here has put you and your mother in grave danger, and if something happens to one of you because of something as trivial as a grab for power, I would never forgive myself. I hope you can believe me and will consider forgiving me for what I am."

Solomon wasn't entirely sure where he stood on matters concerning his father. Even with this most recent revelation about Solomon's mother, and Alphonse's reasoning for doing what he had done, the two of them weren't on good terms. His mother, however, was a different subject entirely. Solomon would do anything for her, and to save her life he needed his father…and the resources he could provide. Which meant he had to be careful how he played this.

"I don't like this," Bram the Death Angel whispered to Solomon from his rightful place on Solomon's forearm. "Something about this doesn't add up."

"You can't worry about that now," Alani the Hula Girl reminded Solomon from his other forearm. "You have to do what it takes to rescue your mother, even if that means bottling up your resentment."

"Solomon needs to keep his wits about him," Bram said. "Nothing about this is what it seems."

"I agree with that," Alani said. "But part of what makes Solomon a good detective is his willingness to do what it takes to help others. His mother, obviously, should rank at the top of that list."

"Can he trust his father?" Bram asked. "I'm not so sure."

"He doesn't have a choice, Bram," Alani said. "You're always the one who views the world in a negative light. I'm the positive one. We've seen how things turn out when you're the one whispering in Solomon's ear. How about we try it my way for once?"

"Have it your way, but don't say I didn't try to warn you," Bram cautioned the Hula Girl.

"I have to help Mom," Solomon said, silencing both of the voices in his head.

"So you'll forgive me?" Alphonse Sharpe asked. "You'll cut me some slack for the man I have become?"

"An attack dog shouldn't apologize for the fact that he has teeth," Solomon said, deciding to be diplomatic with his response.

"True enough," Alphonse admitted. "But when he bites those closest to him, he must face the consequences for his actions. I pray you will allow me one more chance to right the wrongs I've committed over the years."

"You were never a bad father," Solomon said, hating where this conversation was headed.

"Maybe not," Alphonse said. "But I was never a good one either. Look at what I just did to you."

"I attacked you," Solomon said. "I provoked you."

"Forgive me."

"I need time to process all of this," he said noncommittally. "First, we need to get mom back and stop a cold-blooded serial killer. Then we can talk about possible reconciliation."

"I guess that will have to do for now," Alphonse said, seemingly satisfied with the half-measure.

“It’s the best I’ve got at the moment,” Solomon said as he headed toward the door. “I’ve got to go.”

“Be careful, son.”

Solomon couldn’t remember the last time his father had called him that. It was almost enough to make him want to stay here and hash things out with the old man.

But he knew that his mother needed him, and unlike his father, she had never turned her back on him. Which meant he wasn’t going to turn his back on her either. Not now. Not ever.

CHAPTER 15

When Solomon left his father's house, he went out the front door, rather than sneak back across the lawn and through the break in the fence. An armed escort walked him to a cavernous garage filled with all manner of expensive cars, and handed him the keys to something that wouldn't draw much attention: a black Jeep Wrangler that always stayed parked because the other automobiles in Alphonse Sharpe's fleet were so much more impressive and eye-catching.

Solomon resisted the urge to admire the Rolls Royce, the Ferrari, and the Aston Martin as he walked the length of the garage to get to the Jeep. He didn't want word to get back to his father that he was impressed by anything the old man owned. That would have given Alphonse Sharpe far too much satisfaction, and given the way his ribs felt at the moment, Solomon wasn't ready for that just yet.

The Jeep would work perfectly for what he needed. It had the ability to go off-road, which was a plus, and it had four-wheel drive, which might come in handy if he was really forced to go off the grid. It was a nice ride, but not so nice as to be memorable.

Normally, he wouldn't have accepted any help from his father. But this was a different situation. This wasn't about him or the grudge he carried against Alphonse Sharpe. His mother's life was at stake, which meant he was doing this for her. In a war where he was seriously outgunned, any sort of advantage - however small - was not only welcomed, but necessary. He was playing with the big boys now. In truth, he was in way over his head, but there wasn't time to worry about that.

The thing he wanted to do more than anything was rush right over to Saturn Hills Asylum and start digging for answers. But he had been through a lot and needed some rest. Otherwise, this mission was doomed from the start. If he didn't take a few hours to recover and recharge his batteries, he would be sluggish, tired, and not as sharp as he needed to be in order to succeed in infiltrating the asylum. More than anything, he wanted to go back to his apartment and crash. But first, he had one errand to run before he could even attempt to breach Saturn Hills security.

He drove through town with confidence. The glass was heavily tinted which would keep anyone from spotting him behind the wheel. Furthermore, the police wouldn't be looking for the Jeep, and the sight of it wouldn't arouse any suspicions since it hadn't been reported stolen.

Solomon immediately tensed a little at the thought and cursed his overactive mind for conjuring up such a frightening and completely plausible situation. He prayed that he hadn't misread his father's sincerity about rescuing his mother. All Alphonse Sharpe would have to do to teach his son a lesson was call Police Chief Millington and report the Jeep stolen, and suddenly, every cop in Valley Falls would be hot on his heels.

It was best not to think about that right now. He would have to risk it. He needed transportation, and this was all he had at the moment.

Alphonse Sharpe had a vast network of resources, and a Rolodex full of unsavory underground characters who could provide Solomon access to one of the most secure locations in Valley Falls. But it was better to source this particular service from a vendor that he was familiar with. He wasn't ready to go in as a full-fledged partner with his father on this case just yet. That meant he had to use people he trusted, not people who were Alphonse Sharpe's lap dogs.

Solomon looked at his watch and saw that it was almost 4:00 a.m., which was perfect. By the time he arrived, Jonesy would be at work. It had been a while since he had last seen his old friend, but Jonesy wasn't the kind of guy you wanted to see regularly.

The lights at Jonesy's Donut Emporium were just starting to come on when Solomon pulled into the parking lot. Every day without fail, Jonesy started making donuts at 4 a.m., and by 7 a.m. his cases were filled with powdered, cream-filled, and glazed donuts along with an impressive assortment of bear claws, fritters, eclairs, pastries, and muffins.

Solomon chuckled at the sight of the neon man in the window sitting on top of a stack of donuts. For some reason, he imagined the man was Jonesy, and it suddenly struck him as hilarious. The chuckle snowballed and became a full-throated cackle that quickly turned into a belly laugh. Solomon laughed until the pleasure turned into bolts of pain that traveled downward from his busted ribs into his abdomen. Then, he hissed as the agony in his ribs caused him to cut the laughter short.

He was exhausted. He was hurt. He was medicated. He hadn't bothered to ask Bertram what kinds of pills he had been given. He trusted Bertram infinitely more than his own father, but that didn't mean that the medications he had ingested didn't have certain side effects like drowsiness. He felt loopy, and that fact was starting to manifest itself in strange ways.

Like him imagining Jonesy's mug superimposed on the neon man in the donut shop window.

Solomon knew he needed to get this done quickly before he was too incapacitated to be trusted behind the wheel. He drove around to the back of the donut shop, to the receiving area where all of Jonesy's supplies were usually delivered. He parked the Jeep, got out, walked over to the door at the back of the building, and rang the buzzer.

Almost immediately, Jonesy's gruff booming voice came over a speaker mounted near the back door. "Yeah? What have you got for me today?"

"I got a load of Black Lodge flour for you," Solomon said, making sure to say the correct words.

"Is that so?" Jonesy responded with a note of surprise in his voice.

"Yep, that's what it says here on the label," Solomon said. "Black Lodge flour."

"Sounds good," Jonesy replied. "Give me a minute, and I'll open up."

In truth, there was no such thing as Black Lodge flour, but you had to mention that specific ingredient to let Jonesy know why you were here. No doubt, he was running to his office now and consulting the feed for the closed-circuit camera mounted over the back door to see who was in need of his services. Usually, only those on the wrong side of the law came to Jonesy for help, and a man in his line of work couldn't be too careful.

When the door finally opened up, the man who stood there smiling at Solomon seemed at odds with the deep, boisterous voice that he'd heard through the speaker. It was like catching one of those tiny tree frogs that are capable of making such a tremendous noise.

Solomon looked down at the miniscule man and extended his hand. "Jonesy, how the heck are you?"

"Better than you, I would imagine," the diminutive fellow replied, pumping Solomon's hand three times with a firm grip.

Although Solomon wasn't exactly sure how tall Jonesy was, he would have guessed around four and a half feet. Jonesy wasn't a dwarf, but he wasn't a normal-sized man either. He was the perfect size for a jockey, but somehow, Solomon doubted that Jonesy would ever be involved in something as highbrow as horse racing. Solomon didn't know Jonesy's full name, but that was to be expected. No doubt, Jonesy kept as many details secret about himself as he could since any bit of information, no matter how small, might be used to trace his illegal activities back to him.

Jonesy was dressed in all-white baker's attire with a faint dusting of flour on his collar. His long black hair was pulled back in a ponytail, and his pinky glimmered as the streetlight hit the green stone that was set into the ring he wore. He was an odd fellow, but one that Solomon knew he could trust. He also wasn't a man to be trifled with.

He didn't know exactly what the reason was for Jonesy's stature, but he had learned first-hand that the subject was a touchy one. He remembered the first and only time he had made a crack about Jonesy's height. Jonesy clubbed him in the mouth for it, busting both of his lips and knocking him on his backside. Jonesy didn't like to be reminded that he was a little guy in a big world, and he did whatever it took to make people realize that he was every bit their equal. In his mind, he was just as big as everyone else. Of course, when it came to personality, he was bigger than most.

Thankfully, he and Solomon had moved past the height jokes early on and had formed a sort of uneasy friendship over the years. Now, there was only business to discuss.

"You're in trouble," Jonesy said. "Don't deny it. You wouldn't be here if you weren't."

"Guilty as charged," Solomon said.

"You look like crap," Jonesy said. "Did a bag of hammers fall on you?"

"Very funny," Solomon said. "You know the kind of work I do."

"Cheating boyfriend kicked your butt, eh?" Jonesy said, meaning it as a joke. He stopped laughing when he saw the look on Solomon's face.

"Really?" Jonesy said, whistling. "Hazard of the job, I guess. That'll teach you to quit being a Peeping Tom."

"Like what you do is so much more noble," Solomon said.

"Blah blah blah," Jonesy said. "So, are you going to tell me why you're here, or are you going to sit there and fawn over my natural, boyish good looks?"

"You look like the poster boy for an Abercrombie and Fitch that caters to leprechauns."

Jonesy actually laughed at the joke. A smile on his face was a rarity, and Solomon wasn't sure he had ever seen one there before.

"You're an idiot," Jonesy said with a grin. "You want a donut? There's a batch that's done inside."

"I need a slice of Angel Food Cake," Solomon said.

Jonesy's smile fell, and he studied Solomon carefully. "Man, you really are in deep. Is it that bad, Chief?"

"Like you said, I'm here, aren't I?" Solomon added.

"I see," Jonesy said solemnly.

Angel Food Cake was code for: I need your help with something highly illegal.

Jonesy was a unique individual in that he had experience solving a variety of problems, but his help came at a steep price. Angel Food Cake wasn't on the menu (or at least not the menu that was posted behind the counter), and you had to know to ask for it. In nearly every situation where such a strange request was made, Jonesy would simply wave the customer away unless, of course, he knew you...or unless you had started the conversation by mentioning Black Lodge flour. Both of those things applied to Solomon, so Jonesy ushered him inside where no one could see or hear the conversation they were about to have. They had lots to discuss, and none of what they had to talk about involved any sort of cake, Angel Food or otherwise.

For the most part Jonesy's Donut Emporium looked like a traditional donut shop filled with lighted glass-front cases that displayed the finest pastries in Valley Falls. A few molded plastic tables sat to one side of the entryway – with chairs to match – where those who wanted to have coffee and donuts could sit.

The area behind the counter was taken up largely by a blackboard-style menu board that ran the length of the counter, advertising all of the confections Jonesy was known for.

The back room, similarly, looked mostly as it should have with pallets of flour, sugar, tubs of various types of frostings, a pallet jack with a wobbly wheel, a bunch of stainless-steel baking racks used to cool the donuts after they came out of the fryer, and several boxes of paper sacks that could be used to bag up To-Go orders. However, there were certain elements of the back room that seemed a bit incongruous for a meager donut shop, like security cameras that were mounted in all corners, a heavy door made of industrial steel that had a keypad lock, and a gun safe.

Jonesy held a finger up to his lips, motioning for Solomon to be quiet. Quickly, he entered a code into the keypad mounted on the steel door and ushered Solomon inside a small room filled with a computer terminal and a wall of monitors, all of which displayed feeds from a variety of places around Valley Falls.

"Now, we can talk," Jonesy said. "This room is soundproof. It's my command center."

"You're a regular peeping Tom, not me," Solomon said, gesturing to the bank of screens showing a variety of people who were obviously being surveilled without their knowledge.

"Knowledge is power," Jonesy replied. "The more I know about certain people in this town the more leverage I have over them."

"You're quite the mastermind," Solomon said.

"Enough about me," Jonesy said with the wave of a hand. "What, exactly, do you need?"

"I need to get inside Saturn Hills Asylum, and I need access to everything."

"Ok, good," Jonesy said. "I thought you were going to ask me for something really hard to come by, like the skull of Red Fang, or some plutonium for the nuclear warhead you've been working on in your basement. All you're asking for is a full set of credentials into one of Valley Falls' most difficult places to break in or out of. Piece of cake."

"Angel Food Cake," Solomon said with a wry smile. "Remember?"

Jonesy scowled and paced like a caged animal. It was clear he was thinking about whether or not it was possible to get what

Solomon wanted.

Knowing his friend's weak spot, Solomon pushed the envelope of cash his father had given him into Jonesy's hands.

The little man opened the envelope and thumbed through the bills. His eyes went wide at the amount of money he had been handed, but he quickly tried to play off how impressed he was. "When do you need this to happen?" he asked.

"Yesterday," Solomon said. "That's why I'm paying you so handsomely."

"Right," Jonesy replied in deadpan. "I'll just fire up the ol' flux capacitor, jump in the Delorean, and make it happen."

"So we have a deal?" Solomon said. "I wouldn't ask if it wasn't really important."

"Do you know how many times I've been told that?" Jonesy asked.

"But it's really true this time," Solomon said with a grin.

"Give me til the end of the day," Jonesy said. "I'll leave a key in your mailbox that goes to a storage locker I maintain at Pandora's Boxes. Everything you need will be in there."

"You're a lifesaver," Solomon said. "Really. I mean that."

"Don't thank me yet," Jonesy grumbled. "Wait until I've actually delivered on this crazy demand of yours."

"You're almost as good as people say you are," Solomon said, knowing how much Jonesy loved to have his ego massaged. "There's a reason why you're known as the best."

The little man smirked and tried hard to keep it from turning into a full-blown smile. "I do what I can," he said as he led Solomon out of his command center and back to the parking area behind the store.

"Thanks again," Solomon said as he headed toward the

Jeep. "I'm going home to catch some shut eye and let you get to work."

"You're a gentleman and a scholar," Jonesy said with a bow. "When you awaken from your slumber, dear prince, your treasure will await you. I live to serve."

"I owe you one," Solomon said out the Jeep's window as he started to drive away.

"After this, you may owe me more than one," Jonesy said.

CHAPTER 16

One of the things Solomon had done early on when trying to establish himself as a private detective was to make sure that he could never be traced back to his home. People in his line of work made enemies, and he didn't want to spend twenty-four hours a day looking over his shoulder. That's why the landlord thought he was really a man named Charles Abbott.

Abbott, as far as the world knew, was a sanitation worker who had terrible credit and was forced to pay for everything in cash because he wasn't financially stable enough to open a bank account. Solomon had never been more thankful that he had made that sort of preparation than he was right now. The police wouldn't know to look for him here because there was no record of him living in this place. That simple fact allowed him to close his eyes peacefully on more nights than he could count over the years. A P.I. could never be too careful.

He doubled down on that sentiment by pulling the battery out of his phone and tossing it out the window before he reached his apartment. He pulled the battery out of Rico's phone too but didn't dispose of it. He might need it again before all was said and done. He left the burner phone turned on and active. Nobody besides his father knew about it.

Despite not having to worry about being apprehended at his front door by a bunch of cops, Solomon wasn't sure if he would be able to sleep when he got home. Every bone in his body screamed from the repeated beatings he had endured. His head throbbed. His muscles ached. Yet, moments after he set the alarm on the burner phone his father had given him and he collapsed onto his couch, he was snoring soundly.

He slept like the dead and woke up nearly twelve hours later to the phone's annoying alarm. He yawned and stretched and felt pain in places he had forgotten existed. But his body had done some healing while he was out, and he felt a little better than he had before laying down. As he stumbled to the bathroom, he thought he knew what it felt like to be a hundred years old.

Thinking that his master needed some company first thing, Poe jumped up on the sink and studied him as he peed.

"Do you mind?" Solomon asked, shooing the cat away. The effort of such a minor thing nearly made him fall over. He laughed at himself and then grimaced as a bolt of pain raced up his right side.

"Stupid cat," he muttered as he finished his business.

After splashing his face with water a few times to fully wake up, Solomon set out a can of cat food for Poe. Then he grabbed a soda out of the refrigerator and drank the thing in less than twenty seconds. Once finished, he burped loudly, crushed the can, and threw it into the recycling bin. Then, he headed to the mailbox to see if Jonesy had earned his money.

As Jonesy had promised, a key to a mini storage unit had been left in a brown envelope in his box. Unit 116 had been written on the envelope with black magic marker. Solomon pocketed the key and headed back to his apartment. He was just about to grab the Jeep keys and rush out again when he caught a whiff of himself and remembered that he needed to shower and grab a bite to eat before he set out on the next part of his journey.

"You've got to take care of yourself, Solomon," he muttered, heading back to the bathroom to finish what should have been ritual.

The shower felt heavenly, and Solomon let the hot water pour over him until it ran out. His aching muscles responded splendidly to the heat and steam. Once he was out and dressed, he rummaged through his refrigerator until he found some old Chinese take-out that was starting to grow fur. Disgusted, he snarled and threw it in the trash and decided to have a second go at Take Out Russian Roulette.

The second box he opened was barbecue that smelled funny and looked kind of slimy. He couldn't remember the last time he had even had barbecue. He tossed it as well.

The third box, fortunately, was the charm and contained a couple slices of pizza from three days ago. After thirty seconds in the microwave, he devoured them handily and felt even better than he had after the shower.

His ribs still hurt, and he still felt like a man who had been worked over with a baseball bat. But he downed three more aspirin and took another of the antibiotic pills Bertram had given him. They would do their work soon enough.

Pandora's Boxes was a five-minute drive from his house, and the trip was uneventful. He wasn't sure what he would find when he opened the storage unit, but it seemed he had underestimated Jonesy's skills by a mile. Solomon had thought his source might be able to get him a badge that would allow him to sneak around and gain access to various parts of Saturn Hills. But Jonesy had done him one better and taken steps to make him look the part.

The inside of the prefab metal unit was as Solomon expected it to be: dirty concrete floor, a dank, offensive odor that smelled like moldy cardboard and wet newsprint, and nothing else save for what stood in the corner amongst the breeding shadows. Immediately breaking out into a sweat from the oppressive heat inside the metal storage building, Solomon headed straight for a coat rack on which was hung a complete set of Saturn Hills work attire.

The uniform consisted of loose-fitting scrubs and had the asylum insignia embroidered on both the shirt and pants. The badge showed him as a new hire orderly by the name of Jonah Curtis. His picture had been skillfully photoshopped onto the badge, and Solomon had no doubt that this badge would work wherever it was scanned inside the facility. Not only could he move around freely inside Saturn Hills, but he could do so without arousing suspicion.

Jonesy had pinned a note to the front of the uniform. "Jonesy For President! Did I come through or what? Talk to Thaddeus Mitchell when you get to Saturn Hills. He looks like Lurch from The Addams Family and is the Head Orderly. He's expecting you."

Solomon wasted no time changing out of his clothes and into the scrubs. Jonesy had even chosen the right size. He was that good.

After affixing the badge to the front of his shirt, Solomon climbed back into the Jeep and drove the remainder of the way to Saturn Hills.

He was surprised to see a huge burly man waiting in the parking lot, who waved at him as he neared a parking spot. Jonesy's description of Thaddeus Mitchell was accurate. It was like Lurch from the Addams Family had been forced to wear scrubs. The man was all arms and legs and wore a dead stare set into an impassive face. He looked equal parts menacing and ridiculous.

The thought of a man his size and one of Jonesy's stature trying to close a business deal seemed comical to Solomon, and he couldn't help laughing to himself as he parked the Jeep. Somehow, he imagined Thaddeus was the one bowing to Jonesy's will instead of the other way around.

"Thaddeus, I presume," Solomon said.

"That's me," Thaddeus said. "You don't need to return the favor by introducing yourself. I don't need to know your name. As far as I'm concerned, your name is Jonah. Jonesy told me that I need to make sure you have access to anything and everything you need. Your badge should get you into every place inside Saturn Hills. I made sure of that. You aren't here to kill someone, are you?"

Solomon looked at the man strangely. "No, of course not. What did Jonesy tell you exactly?"

"Not much," Thaddeus admitted. "I'm ok helping you get information. What I'm not ok with is helping you kill someone. It's happened in this place before."

"We're on the same page then," Solomon assured him. "I'm not here to murder anybody. I just need to dig up some information on someone who is connected to the asylum."

"Anybody I might know?" Thaddeus asked. "The quicker this gets done, the less risk involved."

"To be honest, I'm not sure who I'm looking for," Solomon said. "All I know is he goes by the name Serafino, and speaks with a smooth accent. Italian maybe. Sicilian perhaps. I would know his voice if I heard it again. I'm not even sure if Serafino is his actual name. He may have an obsession with angels."

Thaddeus nodded and sighed. "I have an idea about who you might be looking for. Follow me, and I'll take you to him. While you're inside, don't do anything to attract attention to yourself. You're a ghost while you're here. If you see someone coming toward you, duck into a nearby room until they're gone. Avoid other members of the staff at all costs. Avoid patients too. You don't know how to handle them, and some of them can be dangerous if you aren't trained on how to diffuse the situation. Any questions?"

"What do I do if I get into trouble while I'm in here?"

"The short answer is don't. I'll be here tonight, so if something happens I will know. But I don't want to put out any fires. So, stay under the radar and keep your head down. Get the information you need and get out. If that happens, you're happy and I'm happy."

"Fair enough," Solomon said.

"Let's go," Thaddeus said as he headed toward the ominous, towering building.

CHAPTER 17

Saturn Hills Asylum was one of the most iconic locations in Valley Falls. While it was primarily known as a treatment facility for the insane, the sick, and the delusional, it was also a correctional facility of sorts where the deranged and deadly were housed. Some of the most famous Saturn Hills alumni were criminals such as The Judas Killer, The King of Hearts, The Purple Lady, Mr. Mindgame, and The Alchemist. The fact should have alarmed Solomon as he climbed the polished white steps that led inside the facility, but he was actually comforted in a way by the truth that some of Valley Falls' most dangerous inhabitants had spent time here or were currently housed within the marble walls. Someone like the Angelmaker would likely feel right at home here.

The exterior of Saturn Hills was the color of bleached bone. At six stories high with over one hundred rooms, the building looked washed out, sick somehow. In fact, it looked exactly like the kind of place where full-frontal lobotomies and electroshock therapy would be commonplace. It also looked out of place, like it was lost in time. The stucco on the outside of the building was chipped and flaking off in places, and many of the window panes were broken-the result of rocks thrown by mischievous kids. Yet, the bars over all the windows ensured that no one could get out that way. Saturn Hills had been built to help the mentally ill, but nothing about the ominous way its shadows stretched out across the front lawn, engulfing everything in darkness, made it seem like a place of healing. Rather, it looked more like the kind of place you might explore out of curiosity and never be heard from again.

Knowing he couldn't let the jitters he felt get the better of him, Solomon followed Thaddeus inside. Nobody gave him more than a passing glance because he was with the towering orderly. Everyone seemed to know Thaddeus. Although Solomon felt like he could hold his own in most situations, having the big man by his side in such an alien landscape made him feel a bit better.

Thankfully, the interior of Saturn Hills wasn't as dilapidated and ramshackle as the outside. The air carried a strong hint of bleach. The hallways were painted in bright colors and filled with various types of diagnostic machines. The walls were adorned with inoffensive art depicting things like sunflowers, ocean waves, or serene sunsets. Yet, the sounds that filtered from the rooms caused Solomon to tense up and feel more unease than he had outside of the asylum. The place was alive with wailing, singing, shouting, grunts, and groans.

"Sing me a song, Alani," Solomon said to the tattooed hula girl image on his arm. "And sing loud enough to block out what I'm hearing."

Alani did as Solomon requested and sang an island tune that should have been accompanied by ukulele. It was enough to occupy most of Solomon's thoughts.

"I can sing too," Bram said, not wanting to be left out. Solomon nodded in agreement, realizing that Alani wasn't quite loud enough to drown out the sounds of insanity. The two inked figures launched into an impression, strangely enough, of Dolly Parton and Kenny Rogers singing "Islands in the Stream."

Solomon wasn't sure if that was better or worse than the sounds he heard coming from further down the hallway, but it was distracting which was helpful. It was also enough to make him laugh. The irony of giggling at a song being sung by two of his tattoos in a place built to treat mental illness wasn't lost on him. He pushed the implications aside. That was a matter for another day.

He followed Thaddeus closely, and they passed through several checkpoints, all of which were locked and required the scan of a badge to move forward. Solomon's badge worked perfectly in every case. Jonesy had really come through for him.

Solomon did his best to seem cool and at ease, but inside, he was actually a bundle of nerves. His mind was always his worst enemy, and it had done a bang-up job in this instance of conjuring up every worst-case-scenario his imagination could handle.

He envisioned a possibility of his badge not working and being questioned by one of the staff members. He imagined getting jumped by a violent patient and being unable to defend himself after suffering so much physical damage in the last twenty-four hours. He thought about someone from inside recognizing him and knowing that he wasn't who he said he was.

None of those things were likely to happen, but that didn't keep Solomon from thinking about them. He tried to counter those thoughts by remembering the video of his mother, gagged and bound to a chair, helpless to do much more than wait on someone to rescue her. He held the key to her release right now, and he had to keep it together. For her.

He followed Thaddeus down a long hallway, through another set of locked doors, and down another corridor with a sign that announced it as Ward B. Thaddeus abruptly stopped at a particular door. A clipboard hanging beside the door announced that the room held Patient #284732.

"This is where the train stops," Thaddeus said. "I think the guy in this cell might be helpful. His name is Angelo. He fits the description you gave me."

Solomon studied Thaddeus for a moment. "Angelo? That's his name?"

"Yeah, why?"

"As in an angel? This can't just be a coincidence."

"I guess so, man," Thaddeus said, not understanding why Solomon was getting so worked up. "What is it you think he did exactly?"

"There's a good chance he has information about someone who has killed several women over the past year," Solomon said.

Thaddeus shook his head. "You may need to reconsider. This guy has been in here for over a year."

"I'm looking for the Angelmaker," Solomon confessed.

Thaddeus didn't seem as shocked by that revelation as Solomon expected. Instead, he thought about the prospect for a moment and finally nodded. "I think he may have some information that will help you. All of this is above my pay grade, but he may be the missing piece to your puzzle."

"Anything special I need to know beforehand?" Solomon said.

"It's better if you go in without knowing anything and form your own opinions."

"Fair enough," Solomon said.

Thaddeus nodded and handed him a walkie talkie. "I'm the only person this will communicate with. If you need me, call."

"Will do," Solomon said.

"I'm going to prepare you in advance," Thaddeus said. "It's weird in there. But Angelo isn't violent, so you should be fine."

"Noted," Solomon said. "Do I just scan my badge to get in?"

Thaddeus nodded again. "Having that badge is like having the keys to the kingdom. It will get you into any place that requires a scan. Don't make me sorry I accepted this job from Jonesy."

"Thanks. I won't. You don't have anything to worry about."

"I'll see you soon then," Thaddeus said, walking away before Solomon could respond.

CHAPTER 18

Solomon stepped into Angelo's cell not really knowing what to expect. Thaddeus had described it as weird, but the word didn't do it justice. The room wasn't padded because Angelo hadn't shown any violent tendencies. Instead, the walls were made of whitewashed cinder blocks. The room, however, was anything but white. Someone had thought it a good idea to furnish Angelo with art supplies, and he had used them liberally on every available square inch of space.

It was the Sistine Chapel as painted by a madman. The images on the walls were frescoes that featured angels fighting angels, angels having their wings ripped off by rebel angels, angels being thrown out of Heaven, fallen angels, choirs of angels, and angels with savage weapons. The moment Solomon saw the nature of what was painted on the walls he was certain he had come to the right place.

Angelo sat on the bed. He had a head full of unruly black hair and a black beard to match. He was of medium build and height. At first glance there was nothing extraordinary about the man, but when he looked up from his sketchpad which he had been drawing on, his brilliant blue eyes were so bright that it would have been easy to accept that he could see the future through them.

"What is it now?" he asked, exasperated. "Somebody just came by thirty minutes ago to make sure I took my meds. How am I supposed to get any work done with you guys coming in and out all the time?"

"Angelo, I'm here to talk to you, not to make sure you took your meds," Solomon said.

"Talk about what?" Angelo asked.

"Angels," Solomon said, hoping the single word would be enough.

Angelo didn't look up, but he answered nonetheless. "Then I looked and heard the voice of many angels, numbering thousands upon thousands, and ten thousand times ten thousand."

"So, you know about them?"

Angelo continued with his sketch, but replied, "I looked up and there before me was a man dressed in linen, with a belt of fine gold from Uphaz around his waist. His body was like topaz, his face like lightning, his eyes like flaming torches, his arms and legs like the gleam of burnished bronze, and his voice like the sound of a multitude."

"I'm impressed," Solomon said. "You do know about angels. Do you know of any that commit murder?"

This last question was enough to finally get Angelo's complete attention. He sat up straight on the bed and put his sketchpad down. Solomon couldn't help noticing that Angelo had been in the middle of drawing a scene with Lucifer being cast out of Heaven by God. Even using such a simplistic medium as pencil drawing for such a complex subject, it was obvious that Angelo was a master of his craft. The details were wrought with a prodigy's touch, and even though the sketch was incomplete, it was better than a lot of the finished art Solomon had seen.

"Why do you ask such a question?" Angelo asked.

"I was told you're an expert on angels of all sorts, even the killing kind," Solomon said.

"Angels are used for God's purposes. Some have been known to kill at the Lord's command."

"Then you have a working knowledge of all angels, even those?"

"I know more than most," Angelo said.

"How is it that you've come to acquire so much knowledge?"

"Simple," Angelo said. "I've met them before. That's why I'm locked up in here. People don't believe in miracles anymore, and anybody who has experienced a miracle is instantly believed to be crazy."

Solomon was just about to speak again when Angelo cocked his head. He looked like a dog listening to the sound of an ultrasonic whistle. He nodded his head and grunted as if in reply to an unheard voice.

At last, he turned back toward Solomon. "You don't really work for the asylum."

Solomon wasn't exactly sure how to respond to this. In the end, he decided to be honest. If the situation called for it, he was certain he could be more convincing than a patient in a mental hospital.

"You're correct. I don't. I needed to speak to you though."

Angelo paused to listen to someone or something again. Try as he might, Solomon couldn't hear anything. The fact was irrelevant to Angelo who obviously could.

"You're here about dead girls," Angelo said.

"Who is talking to you?" Solomon asked.

"Her name is Omniel," Angelo said. "She tells me things. She came to Earth during The Fall."

"She's a fallen angel?"

Angelo nodded. "Yes, but she regretted the decision to rebel and has been looking for ways to atone ever since."

"She thinks that helping you is part of the atonement process?"

"She knows that I'm the key to something big. By guiding me to do the right thing, she can help save a lot of lives."

"Is that so?" Solomon asked.

"I know who has been killing those girls," Angelo said.

"And you're willing to tell me?"

"Omniel says I should, and I believe her."

"So, who has been doing all of the killing?"

Angelo smiled. "Think about it. My name should help. Omniel tells me you're a detective of some sort. If you're really that good, then you should be able to figure this out."

Solomon considered the name 'Angelo.' It was Italian for Angel. A thought occurred to Solomon, but he was certain it couldn't be that simple. Surely not. The Angelmaker made angels. Was it possible he made this one too?

"By any chance, is your father named Serafino?" Solomon asked.

Angelo smiled and whispered something to his unseen companion. He covered his mouth while the two of them chatted back and forth.

"Omniel told me you were smart. Serafino is my father's name. He's the one who put me in this place. I found out he killed the first girl, and he was afraid I was going to turn him in. The easiest thing for him to do was to have me committed. He could discredit me, get me out of the way, and manage to keep me safe all at the same time."

"Is Serafino your father's real name?"

"Yes," Angelo replied. "If you do enough digging, you might think he's just as crazy as you think I am. People in our family are born with the gift of being able to talk to angels. He's no exception. My grandmother named him that because of the ability that passed down from her to him."

Solomon stopped to think about the implications of this for a moment. He wasn't sure he believed everything Angelo was telling him, but there was likely some truth buried in the delusions. "I would think having the ability to communicate with angels would be a deterrent to cold-blooded murder."

"In some cases, it would be," Angelo replied. "But it depends on the kind of angel you talk to. I was fortunate to make a friend in Omniel. Omniel made a mistake millennia ago but is trying to atone. The angels my father talks to aren't interested in repentance."

Solomon nodded as if he understood, but he really didn't. "Do you want out of this place?"

"Wouldn't you?" Angelo asked. "Until a year ago, I had a good life. Then, I saw what I wasn't supposed to see, and my father got rid of me. I would do anything to get out of here, but if I ever did escape, I'm sure he would do whatever it took to silence me. I'm sure none of that makes sense to you. Most people don't have the kind of relationship with their father that I do."

Solomon laughed. "My father hasn't ever committed me to a mental institution, but I still feel like I have a lot in common with you when it comes to father-son relationships. What if I told you that I could help you get out of this place permanently?"

Angelo didn't answer straightaway. Instead, he spoke in a series of whispers to Omniel. "You want me to betray my father," he said at last.

"You were going to turn him in before anyway," Solomon said. "More girls have died since that first one. They could have been saved if you had made it to the police before your father made it to you."

"My father is an evil man," Angelo said. "I'll gladly tell you everything I know. The only problem here is that no one will believe me. I've been diagnosed with paranoid schizophrenia. The doctors think I suffer from delusions. Anything I say about my father will get dismissed immediately as the ramblings of a crazy person."

Solomon considered that for a moment. "Do you think your father loves you?"

It was an odd question and one that seemed to catch Angelo off guard. He consulted with Omniel again before answering. "I don't know the answer to that, but Omniel seems sure that my father loves me. That's why he had me thrown in here instead of killed. He couldn't bear to think about harm coming to me, but he also couldn't bear to think of harm coming to himself either. A yearlong trip to sunny Saturn Hills was the solution that fixed all of that."

"Would you be willing to try something risky to help get your father off the streets?" Solomon asked as a seed of an idea began to sprout inside his mind.

"Will it get me out of here so I can pursue my art in the way it deserves to be pursued?" Angelo asked.

"It will," Solomon told him. "And I can guarantee that I know a patron who will support your art in exchange for helping take Serafino down."

"Then I will help you," Angelo said. "But not only will you have my assistance, you will also have the help of an angel of the Lord."

"The more the merrier," Solomon said. "Let's go."

CHAPTER 19

This time, when Solomon used Rico's phone to call Serafino, he did so knowing that he had the upper hand. Gone was the oily knot in his stomach. For the first time since all of this mess had started, he wasn't behind the eight ball.

"Mr. Sharpe, I honestly didn't expect to hear from you again so soon," Serafino said in a voice that was silky smooth. "To what do I owe the pleasure?"

"Don't talk, Serafino," Solomon said. "Just listen carefully. I have someone here that wants to talk to you."

Solomon quickly switched the phone to speakerphone mode and offered the device to Angelo.

"Dad?" Angelo said in a strained voice. "It's me."

"Angelo?" Serafino replied. Solomon was fairly certain that most things didn't surprise the Angelmaker, but this phone call had done exactly that.

"Somehow this man found me," Angelo said. "The things he's done to me…"

"Son?" Serafino said as a note of panic crept into his voice. "I thought you'd be safe in Saturn Hills. I specifically instructed them not to hurt you, to make you comfortable, to provide anything you needed. I never imagined anyone else would find you there."

Solomon nodded to Angelo and took the phone back. He turned the speakerphone option off and put the device back against his ear. "Here's how this is going to work," Solomon said. "You will meet me tonight at midnight at the Lamplight Theatre. You will come alone."

"Or else what?" Serafino asked. A little of the old confidence had returned to his voice.

Solomon motioned for Angelo to hand him his sketchpad and pencil. He quickly wrote the word 'scream' down and showed it to Angelo.

Playing his part perfectly, Angelo wailed horribly, making it sound like he was being boiled alive. "Please stop," Angelo wept, improvising a bit and seeming to enjoy the theatrics of it all.

Solomon put the phone back up to his ear. "Or else I will make an angel of my own. Do you have any other questions?"

"Just one," Serafino said coolly. "What do you think I will do to you once the cops apprehend you and bring you to me? It will be something painful. I can promise you that. A huge chunk of the force works for me, you know? You've chosen the wrong day to make a stand."

Somewhere in the distance came the faint wailing of police sirens. Solomon guessed they were a mile or so away. He had to give Serafino credit for one thing: the man had the police trained to respond immediately when he snapped his fingers. It was yet another of the reasons why the Angelmaker hadn't been captured so far.

"Maybe I will skin you alive," Serafino said. "Or maybe I'll throw you to my dogs and let them eat you in small bites. Or maybe I will kill you by degrees, torturing you first so I can enjoy the sound of your screams."

Through the side window of the Jeep, Solomon watched the police storm Saturn Hills Asylum. Angelo's eyes went wide at the sight of so many officers.

"Oh, I'm sorry," Solomon said. "You really thought I would just wait at Saturn Hills until the cops showed up? I'm not that careless. I'm somewhere else now. Angelo is with me and will remain so until midnight tonight. If you show up and do exactly what I tell you, then there's a chance he will live to see tomorrow. If you try anything funny, I will make you remember the day that you squared off against me and lost. Do you understand?"

"You're making a grave mistake, Mr. Sharpe," Serafino said through what sounded like gritted teeth. "I'm not the kind of enemy you want."

"Are we on the same page?" Solomon asked. "I'd really like to finish up this call."

Serafino answered cryptically. "Then one of the seraphim flew to me, having in his hand a burning coal that he had taken with tongs from the altar."

"I'll be sure to bring a fire extinguisher," Solomon said. "See you tonight. None of your cop buddies are welcome either. Come alone."

And with that, he disconnected the call, put the Jeep in gear, and drove slowly away from the mental institution. In the rearview mirror, the asylum reminded him of an anthill that has been jabbed with a sharp stick. Police officers raced in and out the front entrance with guns drawn, their movements coordinated by a powerful and devious puppet master who had a penchant for murdering young girls. The whole place was chaotic with activity, and Solomon couldn't help thinking that this very moment was the safest time to commit a crime virtually anywhere in Valley Falls. The entire police force seemed to have converged on Saturn Hills, leaving the rest of the city unmonitored.

But Solomon knew that wasn't entirely true. There was at least one cop out there that wasn't part of this, and it was time to give him a buzz.

Detective Wallace Hammett picked up on the second ring. "Hammett speaking," he said, apparently not recognizing the number that had called him.

"Detective, this is Solomon Sharpe."

"Good Lord, Sharpe, you've got every cop in the city looking for you. They want your head on a pike. You've certainly made some big enemies in a short amount of time."

"Tell me about it," Solomon said. "I need some information and possibly a favor."

"How can your humble servant be of assistance?" Hammett said, not bothering to hide the sarcasm in his voice.

"First off, tell me what happened at Arcane Infinity."

"A sniper took out the desk clerk and managed to hit the owner, Peter Silverstone, in the shoulder. I'm pretty sure the shooter was the same one who killed your bouncer friend at The Carbon Underground. I think someone is trying to pin all of this on you. They knew your car was abandoned in the magic store parking lot. They also knew you escaped my custody and were a person of interest in the first shooting."

"Definitely sounds like a frame job to me," Solomon said. "I'm innocent."

"Maybe," Hammett said with a laugh.

"So, Silverstone is still alive?" Solomon asked.

"Alive and kicking. He was patched up and sent home. His buddy wasn't so lucky. He's sitting in one of the meat lockers down at the morgue."

"I had nothing to do with any of that," Solomon said a little more seriously this time.

"I know," Hammett said. "Remember, I'm on your side here. I know what you're up against."

"Sorry," Solomon said. "I just feel like I need to be protesting my guilt loudly since so many people are looking for me. Anyway, back to the favor. Can you get a message to Silverstone?"

Hammett seemed surprised by the request. "Sure, I suppose I can."

"Ok, great," Solomon said. "I'm going to text you the message when we hang up. It's imperative that you convince him to agree to what I'm going to ask."

"Is that all?" Hammett said, sounding a little perturbed that he was being used as an errand boy.

"Just one other thing," Solomon said. "Be at the Lamplight Theatre a little before midnight and make sure you look presentable. You may end up on camera before the night is over. If things go the way I hope they will, you're going to be the man who captures the Angelmaker. Make sure to stay hidden until I give the signal."

"I sure do hope you know what you're doing, Sharpie," Hammett sighed. "If you're wrong about all of this, you and I are both going to end up in pine boxes."

"Trust me," Solomon said. "This will work."

"And you know this how?" Hammett asked.

"Simple. I kidnapped the Angelmaker's son from Saturn Hills Asylum and am holding him hostage in exchange for a meeting with the man."

Hammett fell silent for a moment while he digested the information he had just been given. "Maybe I shouldn't ask any further questions. Text me the information you want me to give to Silverstone. I'll see that he gets it."

"See you tonight," Solomon said before hanging up.

As Solomon ended the call, he noticed Angelo staring at him with a look of deep-seated concern. "You seem very confident," he said. "You don't know my father. He will show up. But what he does when he gets there is another story. He will burn anything and everything down that gets in the way of him getting what he wants, and I can guarantee right now he wants you more than anything else in the world."

"Oh, he's going to get me," Solomon said. "With both barrels."

CHAPTER 20

The Lamplight Theatre was one of the premier venues for live entertainment in Valley Falls. It hosted plays, orchestras, the occasional comedian, musicals, and magicians, allowing a variety of performers to earn their living by showcasing their skills to a willing audience.

In addition to being one of the most popular hotspots for patrons of the arts, the building was also one of the most historic in Valley Falls. Having been constructed in 1890, and renovated several times over the last century, the Lamplight Theatre was a sight to behold with its brocade draperies, crystal chandeliers, gilded moldings, and Wurlitzer organ. It was a place of grand performances, and if Solomon had his way, tonight would continue that tradition.

Alphonse Sharpe was on the Lamplight Theatre's Board of Directors, so gaining access to the building wasn't a problem. The only thing, in fact, that would be problematic is if Serafino failed to show up.

Solomon checked his watch a couple minutes before midnight as he paced nervously behind the crimson velvet curtain. He still wasn't sure how this was going to go down, but he hoped it would all work out for the best. It had to.

For his part, Angelo sat in a chair beneath the glow of a high-powered spotlight near the front of the auditorium. His arms and legs were bound to the chair. His mouth was covered with duct tape, and his gaze darted erratically from one side of the stage to the other. He seemed worried about how things were going to go down, and based on everything he had said about the kind of monster his father truly was, his fears were well-founded.

When the clock struck twelve, Solomon took a deep breath and prepared to give the performance of a lifetime. "Angelmaker," he shouted. "Show yourself if you are here."

Not one to miss his cue, a tall, thin man appeared at the other end of the theatre. He had a hawkish face and slicked-back black hair. The skin on his face was stretched tight over his skull, giving him a vaguely cadaverous look. He wore a gray suit and a wine-colored shirt with no tie. He looked like the Grim Reaper on his way to a cocktail party. He carried a machete that gleamed and shimmered in the lights.

"Serafino Bartoli, I presume," Solomon said.

"In the flesh," the man said in a lilting voice that seemed incapable of coming from the mouth of a killer. "Let my son go if you know what's good for you."

"I've learned a lot about you since I kidnapped Angelo," Solomon said, buying himself a few extra seconds to get into position. "The reason you aren't on anyone's radar in Valley Falls is because you don't actually live in Valley Falls. You're from Crowley's Point. That's brilliant, actually."

"I've always been told it's unwise to foul your own nest," Serafino said. "It's easier to foul someone else's nest and then go back home where it's nice and safe."

"Of all the things I thought you might do for a living, dealing in rare and antique books was not on my list of guesses," Solomon told the man.

"I'm sorry to disappoint," Serafino said. "I considered opening a winery once, but getting rich at that involves selling millions of bottles of wine. With books, I can track down one that's highly sought after and sell it to the highest bidder. It's a lot less work actually, if you're good at what you do...and I am. You wouldn't believe how much money I made on a copy of *The Gutenberg Bible*. More than enough money, I think, to cover up whatever I end up doing to you. Maybe I'll skin you alive and wear you like a coat."

"You should stop talking now," Solomon said, stepping behind Angelo's chair. With a flick of the wrist, he pulled out a knife that he pressed tight against Angelo's throat. "Turn yourself over to the authorities, and I'll let him live. This isn't a negotiation. It's a demand that you will meet, or else."

Serafino laughed. "You have too many scruples for killing. You won't hurt Angelo. I'm confident of that. Men like me have no issue spilling blood. Men like you are unable to do so."

Solomon pressed the knife into Angelo's neck, pricking the skin. Angelo whimpered. A tiny rivulet of blood ran down his throat. "Are you so sure of that?" Solomon asked. "This ends tonight."

"On that we both agree," Serafino said as he jammed the machete into a sheath on his belt and pulled a lighter out of one of his pockets. "Maybe the machete wasn't sufficient to grab your attention. I think I have a better idea that might make you a little more enthusiastic about doing what I say."

With a quick flick of his thumb, a blue flame appeared. He waved the lighter around, pretending to lose his grip on it. He fumbled a bit with it before grabbing it securely again to hold it out in front of him. "I'm so clumsy sometimes," he said.

"You are threatening to start a fire," Solomon said, clearly unimpressed. "Nothing changes."

"If you don't let my son go, I will burn this place to the ground, and you will go up in flames. I've taken the liberty of securing all of the exits. The one behind me is the only one that is open. To get out you will have to go through me. This only ends one way, and I control it."

"You only have one chance to snuff that lighter and surrender yourself to me," Solomon said.

"You aren't as smart as I thought you were," Serafino said. "If I set this place ablaze, you will die here. I will make sure of it."

"Your son will die too," Solomon reminded him. "I'll make sure of that."

"If he dies, he dies," Serafino said.

Angelo's eyes went wide when he heard it. The entire plan was built around the tiny possibility that Serafino actually loved his son and wouldn't allow harm to come to him.

"I think you're bluffing," Solomon said, pressing the knife harder against Angelo's throat. Angelo groaned.

Serafino shifted the lighter from one hand to the other. "Am I?"

"I guess we're about to find out," Solomon said as he ripped the knife across Angelo's throat. Blood sprayed from the wound in a crimson arc, and Angelo's head dropped immediately.

"No!" Serafino shouted, dropping the lighter.

CHAPTER 21

Almost immediately, the plush carpet caught fire, and a blaze began to spread, licking up the walls, devouring the seating on the back row, and spreading to the aisles. Solomon moved away from Angelo and watched as a weeping Serafino raced to his son. Serafino did, in fact, love Angelo after all, and he wailed at the bloody sight of the boy, gagged and bound to the chair.

He didn't chase Solomon, and he didn't worry about the fire. Instead, he climbed to the top of the stage, hoping to save his son's life before he bled out. The look in the man's eyes was one of red-eyed panic. It was the first human reaction he had shown, and for the briefest of moments Solomon felt sorry for him. Then he remembered what Serafino had done to five daughters in his quest to entertain himself by "making angels", and the feeling was short-lived.

Serafino deserved any misery that came his way.

Yet, something happened when Serafino reached the top of the stage where his son sat slumped and bloody in the straight-backed chair. One moment, Angelo was there, and the next he wasn't. Serafino whirled around in confusion and rage as he spotted the various mirrors positioned on the floor and at several places around the stage. He realized too late that all of this was a magician's trick. He had been hoodwinked, and nothing brought that revelation home more than the trap door on stage opening up beneath him and swallowing him whole.

Serafino screamed out in rage before disappearing.

"Hammett!" Solomon shouted to the detective who was waiting in the wings. Wallace was already rushing out and shouting expletives into his phone to the fire chief. Meanwhile, the Lamplight Theatre was going up in smoke around them.

Solomon raced toward Angelo, but Peter Silverstone was already there, untying him and helping him to his feet. What would have normally been a simple act of undoing a few knots was made more difficult for the magician by the sling that he wore on one arm. Within seconds, he had Angelo freed completely, but the effort made him grimace as the pain from the gunshot he had suffered the day before spread up his arm.

Still, despite the misery dealt to his wounded limb, Silverstone was smiling. "The prop knife worked perfectly," he said to Angelo.

"You are as good as your father," Angelo said. "Your dad is considered a hero in Valley Falls.

"Thank you," Peter said.

"Uh, guys, we need to get moving," Solomon said with a note of concern in his voice. "Don't forget this place is on fire."

"There is a large air vent toward the rear of the theatre that you can use to get out of here," Hammett said. "It's an access point that the contractors were supposed to wall up after the Lamplight upgraded their air conditioning system, but they missed it. It's not on the new plans because it was supposed to be eliminated. I'm pretty sure Serafino missed it because most people don't know it's still there. The theatre hung a huge painting of some Greek god over it to hide it. The vent is big enough to crawl through, and you should be able to use it to get to the alleyway behind the theatre. Don't ask me how or why I know this. It's a long story. Find the vent and get out of here. There will be enough questions that I have to answer about this case after the fact without having to explain how and why you and Angelo are involved."

"You're sure?" Peter asked. "What about the two of you?"

"We will be fine. Now go!" Hammett said, waving the two of them away.

The detective waited until they were both gone before turning back to Solomon. "We really caught him, didn't we?" he said, motioning to the trap door. "I'm about to make the biggest arrest of my career."

"There's a cage under that trap door," Solomon said. "He should have fallen right into it. All you have to do now is go and get him."

In the distance, the wail of fire engine sirens cut through the night. The Lamplight Theatre's sprinkler system had failed to completely activate (likely because of something Serafino had done to tamper with it before entering the building). However, some of the sprinklers had gone off which was the only reason that the fire hadn't completely spread to all parts of the old building. The air was thick with smoke and the cloying smell of old varnish crackling and peeling off the antique seating. The flames were steadily creeping forward from the back of the theatre toward the stage.

"I need to get cuffs on our culprit," Hammett said. "With a huge portion of the force in his pocket, I can't risk one of the bad apples compromising my arrest."

"I'll help you," Solomon said, following Hammett toward the stage. "Let's get this done and get out of here before this place burns to the ground with us inside."

"Roger that," Hammett said as he lifted the trap door and peered into the cage that had been positioned atop the platform beneath. Much to their surprise, the cage door hung askew, and the cage itself was empty.

"No!" Hammett hissed. "He must have picked the lock."

"Wait, look," Solomon said, pointing to blood on some of the bars. "He must have fallen on that machete he was waving around earlier and injured himself in the fall. We can still catch him."

"Let's go!" Hammett said, jumping down into the hell mouth. Solomon followed.

The space beneath the stage was filled with theatre junk. In places it was difficult to move around because of all the cross beams and bracing that helped support the stage. It was like walking into your child's bedroom and marveling at how clean everything is until you look under the bed and see the ugly truth. Yet there was a path that wound its way in and around the heaps of junk if you knew where to look. A trail of blood droplets marked the path clearly enough, showing where Serafino had gone.

As they crawled on hands and knees under the stage, desperate to find the path that Serafino had taken, the smoke grew thicker and heavier which meant the fire was growing. The fire engines were close enough that they were screaming now, and it was likely that firemen were on the scene with their hoses and their good intentions. But none of them knew what had happened inside, and they might inadvertently help Serafino escape without even realizing that they were aiding a serial killer. To them, he might simply seem like another victim that needed help getting out of a burning building.

"It looks like he headed toward the dressing rooms," Solomon said, pointing out a streak of red that snaked out from beneath the stage and ended at the doorway leading to the back hallway where all of the performers dressed and prepared.

Hammett did a duck walk toward the open space at the edge of the stage and staggered out, straightening up before pulling his gun. Solomon crawled out after him and groaned as every injury from the past two days cried out in unison.

The blood did, in fact, head toward the door leading to the dressing rooms, but another streak veered off at the last minute toward the space reserved for set building and for storing all the old sets.

Hammett looked around in confusion, cursing under his breath. "Where did he go?" he said impatiently.

"The door handle isn't bloody," Solomon said, pointing. "He didn't go through that door. He headed toward set storage and set building."

"Good eye," Hammett said, changing course at the door to head away from the dressing rooms and move into a large area behind the stage where all of the sets from various productions were kept. Solomon didn't consider himself to be a huge theatre junkie, but he didn't have any trouble picking out a backdrop of the Swiss Alps from *The Sound of Music*, a bandshell used in *The Music Man*, a scene of the Royal Palace of Siam taken from *The King and I*, and a beautiful castle setting from *Cinderella.*

"Careful," Solomon said, creeping carefully along to avoid making a sound. "He could be anywhere back here."

"Yeah, but where?" Hammett asked.

Serafino answered the question with a shout, rushing out from behind a backdrop from *My Fair Lady*. With a roar, he hurled a claw hammer, hitting Hammett in the chest with a dull thud.

Hammett went down instantly.

Serafino charged Solomon, burying his head into Solomon's ribs. It was the sort of move that an offensive lineman might use against an opponent to make a hole for his linebacker to run through, and Serafino pushed with everything he had. The two men crashed into a large windmill from the last production of *Don Quixote*. The structure fell over on top of the two with a loud thud, splintering into pieces. The added weight of the set crashing down on them didn't stop Solomon and Serafino from grappling with each other and doing their best to get a hold on the other.

Solomon's body screamed out in pain.

Serafino was the bigger of the two men and used his size to his advantage, knocking Solomon down before leaping on top of him. He used his extra weight and rested his knees on Solomon's shoulders.

Solomon grabbed a stray piece of broken lumber from the toppled windmill. He swung the wood like a club, striking Serafino in the side of the head.

The big man fell over, grabbing at his temple. His hand came away red, and the sight of his own blood seemed to awaken something primal in him that made his eyes light up with a primitive sort of fire most often seen in the savage man of early civilization. He roared as he got to his feet, enraged.

Solomon scurried to his feet and swung the stick again, this time hitting Serafino in the side, knocking the wind out of him.

Serafino grabbed the two-by-four as it struck him. With a considerable bit of effort, he wrenched the lumber away from Solomon and tossed it to the side. Then, he pulled the machete out of its sheath and held it out in front of him, shifting it from hand to hand, testing its weight. The tip of the blade was bloody, and Solomon saw that the blade had actually punched through the sheath during the fall and stabbed Serafino in the thigh. That was where the blood in the cage and beneath the stage had come from. The right leg of his trousers was wet with a considerable amount of blood. From the look of things, it was very possible that he had nicked something important, and if that was true, then all Solomon had to do was stay alive long enough to allow the Angelmaker to bleed out.

Yet, animals are most deadly when wounded, and Serafino seemed more beast than man. He staggered on his feet, but seemed steady enough with the machete.

"I will not be beaten by you," he hissed. With a roar, he swung the machete in a wide arc.

Solomon dodged and then felt a burning sensation in his abdomen. He looked down to see his own blood trickling down his stomach from a shallow cut.

Serafino laughed and swung the blade again. The machete missed him by inches, and Solomon couldn't help thinking that this was likely the very blade that the Angelmaker had used to kill and dismember five young women. This knife had a taste for killing.

As the two of them circled each other, looking for the right opening to attack, Solomon nearly tripped over something and glanced down long enough to see that it was the edge of a painter's tarp that had somehow gotten dragged out during their fight amongst the various sets. He scooped it up and whirled it like a rope. The canvas tarp was heavy. When Serafino tried to slash Solomon the blade bounced off the tarp harmlessly.

Solomon whipped it again, and this time it wrapped itself around the blade, becoming entangled. Solomon pulled like a master angler yanking on the line at precisely the right time to lodge the hook in the fish's mouth. The machete flew out of Serafino's hand and slid across the concrete floor.

Before Serafino could pivot and plot any sort of new strategy, Solomon tossed the tarp at him, confusing him momentarily. Those couple of seconds were all he needed to tackle the big man and drive him onto the floor. Serafino thrashed and fought, but his arms were caught up in the tarp. Solomon punched his enemy in the head, landing blow after blow until eventually the Angelmaker went still.

Solomon wasn't sure whether the man was simply unconscious or dead, but he was out of commission which was all that mattered.

By now the firemen had broken into the Lamplight and were busy putting out the fires. Much of the theatre was damaged and would have to be completely gutted before any performances could take place there again. However, those few sprinkler heads that malfunctioned might have been the only thing that saved the entire building from going up in smoke. Had they not gone off despite Serafino's tampering and made a wet barrier that slowed the fire long enough for the firemen to arrive on scene, the damage might have been much, much more severe.

Hammett, for his part, still wasn't moving, and Solomon was scared to think that his only ally in this case might be dead and unable to speak up on his behalf. He knelt beside Hammett and pressed his fingers against the man's neck. The detective had a pulse and was breathing on his own. Solomon followed that by checking Serafino's neck for a pulse and discovered that he was still alive as well.

Afraid that Serafino might somehow miraculously give them

the slip again, Solomon raced over to a nearby workbench where various parts of the stage sets were constructed and found a roll of duct tape. Serafino was already entangled in the tarp, and Solomon made sure he would be unable to free himself any time soon by taping the man's ankles and wrists together.

Now, confident that he could help Hammett without worrying about his enemy making a recovery and getting the jump on him, Solomon went to the detective and shook the man by the arm. "Detective," he said. "Detective."

Hammett didn't move at first. Although he was alive, it was still unclear what sort of damage he had suffered from the flying hammer. "Come on, wake up," Solomon said, shaking him harder.

The detective's eyes fluttered like the wings of butterflies, and he muttered something unintelligible.

"Detective!" Solomon said, shaking him harder.

Hammett opened his eyes like a man waking up from anesthetic. He muttered something again.

"What did you say?" Solomon asked, getting closer to the detective to try and make out his words.

"I'm...wearing...body armor," Hammett managed. "Hurts like a mother. But I'll live. Hitting my head when I went down will be the most serious thing I have to deal with."

"Can you sit up?" Solomon asked.

Hammett nodded slowly and took Solomon's hand. With some effort he managed to get upright, and then he staggered to his feet.

"Did he get away?" Hammett asked, looking around in a daze.

"Nope," Solomon said, pointing to the shape under the tarp. "We got him."

Hammett shook his head from side to side to clear out the

cobwebs. "Then, let's march this sicko out and parade him in front of the world."

Solomon smiled. "There may be a reporter or two waiting outside. Someone may have called them earlier with an anonymous tip. I'd make sure Serafino's face is uncovered and visible. The reporters will do all the dirty work for you. Once his identity gets out, nobody will stick their neck out for him. They won't want the heat that comes from being associated with him. This is the end of the line for the Angelmaker."

"And what about you?" Hammett asked.

"I'm getting out of here," Solomon said. "I'm sure you can clear everything up and make sure I'm no longer considered a suspect. In the meantime, I have some other related business to attend to."

"I owe you one, Sharpie," Detective Hammett said.

"Don't worry," Solomon said with a smile. "One of these days I'll collect."

CHAPTER 22

Solomon had left the Jeep parked two blocks away and was grateful for the time it took to get back to it. He had inhaled a good bit of smoke, and his lungs seemed to sigh in relief with each gulp of cool night air. He only hoped no one saw him on the way because, frankly, he was a mess. The entire front of his shirt was bloody. He was covered in bruises. His clothes were disheveled. He looked like he had just crawled out of a wrecked car.

"Well, you did just survive a fight with a serial killer," Bram, the death angel on his right forearm, told him. "I have to say I'm impressed. I didn't think you had it in you. You're more formidable than I gave you credit for."

"You're a depiction of death," Solomon reminded him. "It's not surprising which outcome you were hoping for. Nothing would make you happier than getting to reap me."

"I'm not sure that's true," Bram said, feigning offense. "Just think about the implications of what you're saying."

"It does bring up an interesting question," Alani, the hula girl on his other forearm, interjected. "If you have a depiction of death on your arm that somehow lives in your mind, then it has life in a way. If you were to die in reality, then that version of death would also die. Can death die? And if so, wouldn't it be in Bram's best interest for you to stay alive?"

"That is not dead which can eternal lie, and with strange

aeons even death may die," Solomon said. "If anybody understood the weird and wacky, it was H.P. Lovecraft, and the way I feel right now, I believe every word he ever wrote. I read a ton of that stuff as a teenager. I guess a little of it stuck with me."

"Even if it's possible, I'm not ready to die yet," Bram said.

Solomon ignored the death angel and focused on the hula girl. "I don't know if Bram is actually alive or has the ability to die. You would fall into that same category. All I know is that I'm not going to focus on staying alive for Bram's sake...or for yours. I'm going to stay alive because I want to live. Emily needs me, and I plan on sticking around for her. The two of you have no say in the matter."

"You do realize you're having a three-way conversation right now, and two of the participants involved are tattoos?" Bram reminded him. "You've officially gone crazy. It's bad enough to talk to me or her every now and then. But we've officially crossed over into a whole different level of crazy. Now, you're imagining conversations between your tattoos."

"Shut up, Bram," Alani said as she continued with her never-ending dance in an imaginary Hawaii. "He's hurt worse than he thought. That cut on his abdomen is pretty deep. It's no wonder he's got the two of us talking to each other. Deep down, some part of him knows that the outlook for him is not very good. Maybe he's forcing the two of us to talk to each other in hopes that we will figure out how to keep him alive. His subconscious will have to do the work that his conscious mind isn't capable of doing at the moment."

"It sounds like we're about to get a real-time answer to the question you asked earlier," Bram said, holding his scythe in his skeletal hands as he had since the day he was drawn. "He will die within the hour if he doesn't receive medical attention. I never even considered the notion that I might die too, until now. I'm Death. How can such a thing be possible?"

"Stop thinking about yourself. We can't let him die," Alani said. "Or if you're determined to be selfish, focus on keeping him alive so you don't have to find out the answer to the question of your own mortality."

"You two stop arguing," Solomon said. "I'm not going to die."

"You will if you don't get some medical attention," Alanie told him.

"For once, she and I agree on something," Bram added. "You better get moving."

"I'm fine," Solomon said as he reached the Jeep. But he soon realized the absurdity of his statement. He didn't even remember walking the two blocks to where the Jeep was parked. It was like walking through a fog and emerging suddenly into a clearing. The Jeep was right there in front of him, and he honestly didn't have any recollection of the path he had taken to get to it.

"Better hurry," Bram told him.

Solomon had just started to unlock the door when he felt all of the strength drain out of his legs. He grabbed the door handle with one hand and the luggage rack with the other and used those to hold himself up.

After a couple of deep breaths, he managed to open the door, get inside, and get the Jeep started.

His vision was blurry, and his head felt like it was full of strange, swimming creatures. But he was able to put the Jeep in gear and start driving. The road seemed to move in front of him, shifting from side to side like a slithering snake. He turned on his headlights and realized that they didn't help. Everything in front of him was still extremely dark and fuzzy.

The trip was mostly periods of darkness illuminated with brief fleeting moments of clarity. Those flashes of clear-headedness were the only thing that kept him alive. The streets were pretty empty at this time of night which helped him avoid a collision.

"You're close to your father's house," Alani said in a soothing voice. "All you have to do is make it there. I can see it up ahead. Just another two blocks."

"I'm so sleepy," Solomon said. "I just want to lay down and sleep for a decade or two."

"Don't close your eyes yet," Bram said. "Drive as fast as you can and don't worry about hitting the brakes."

Normally, Solomon would have argued with the snarky death angel, but he was too out of it to do so now. Instead, he did as he was told and pressed down on the accelerator.

"You're going to get him killed," Alani said in a panicked voice.

"Trust me," Bram said. "I know what I'm doing."

Up ahead, the front gates of Alphonse Sharpe's estate were swiftly approaching. They were nasty, formidable, and made of thick wrought iron. Like everything else the elder Sharpe owned, no expense had been spared on them, and they were meant to keep out all sorts of intruders. But, as far as Bram knew (after swimming through Solomon's memories and knowledge banks) no one had ever tried to ram the gates head on.

"Hang on," Solomon said as he raced across the final stretch of road.

The gates rose up quickly before him, and Solomon ran the Jeep into them without a care in the world. Miraculously, the gates held, and the Jeep didn't bust through. The Jeep was a mess of tangled and snarled metal, but the damage to the vehicle didn't matter. Solomon had gotten everyone's attention, and the moment he hit the gate, a host of guards converged on him with guns drawn.

He blacked out after that.

CHAPTER 23

When Solomon opened his eyes, he found himself in bed. He groaned and tried to sit up before realizing that he was hooked up to a variety of machines. An IV needle was taped flat against his arm and was steadily providing a variety of fluids to him via a drip bag.

He looked around in confusion, trying to piece together the last things he could remember.

He was in his father's house. Of that, he was certain. Bits and wispy fragments of memories came back to him from the moments leading up to his arrival at the Sharpe estate: the conversation with Alani and Bram, the blood seeping between his fingers as he tried to keep pressure on the wound that slashed across his abdomen, crashing the Jeep into the gate, getting surrounded by his father's foot soldiers and held at gunpoint until one of them recognized him and called the main house, being rushed in on a stretcher with Bertram anxiously waiting in a makeshift operating room, beeps and blips coming from enough medical equipment to supply a small hospital.

Then, sleep. Glorious sleep.

Solomon ran his hands gingerly over his stomach and wasn't surprised to find that most of his torso was wrapped tightly with bandages. He was pretty certain that he was stitched up beneath the bandages, and he hissed in pain as he touched the area.

"Daddy," Emily said, appearing suddenly beside his bed.

Without waiting for him to say anything, she wrapped her arms around his neck and hugged him fiercely. The hug made him hurt in more places than he had imagined such a gesture could, but he didn't care. Seeing his little girl safe and sound made everything he had gone through worth it.

"Are you ok?" she asked him tenderly. "I've been so worried about you."

"I'll be ok, poodle," he said. "Don't worry about me. I'm tough."

"What happened?" she asked.

Truthfully, Solomon wasn't sure how much he needed to tell her about everything, so he went with the only answer that made sense. "Things are kind of foggy right now," he said. "A lot has happened in the last couple of days that I'm still trying to make sense of. Have you contacted your mother?"

"I did," Emily said. "Granddad bought me a new phone first thing this morning and told me to call mommy."

"I'm sure your mom had a lot of questions about where you've been," Solomon said.

"She couldn't stop crying," Emily said. "She was really worried about me. I assumed you called her after the other night."

"I meant to," Solomon said. "I will clear things up with her as soon as I'm able to get out of this bed."

"Okay, daddy. I love you," Emily said.

Inexplicably, the declaration hit Solomon with a force nothing else had. Maybe it was because of exhaustion. Maybe it was because of the physical damage he had sustained over the past three days. Or maybe he had spent so much time lately trying to be strong and suddenly realized he didn't have to be Superman anymore. Whatever the case, Solomon began to weep openly as some internal dam crumbled, allowing a flood of emotions to wash over him.

It was like the stopper had been pulled on a bathtub. Solomon could feel all of the tensions draining away the more he cried. The tears continued to flow, and he did nothing to stop them. "I love you too, baby," he said.

As Emily was about to leave to go and talk to her friends on her new phone, Solomon asked her for one more hug. She came back and grabbed him fiercely, and he put his arms around her even though the gesture was misery in so many ways. In a strange way, Emily was his anchor to reality, and he clung to her like a victim on the verge of drowning. Everything about Emily was normal and real, and that was what he needed more than anything else. No secret cabals. No serial killers. No cloak and dagger missions ordained by mythical Oz-like characters who hid behind curtains and fake names.

Eventually, Emily left, and Solomon let her.

He was exhausted and had just closed his eyes with the intention of sleeping again when he heard the approach of footsteps.

He opened his eyes to see his father standing over him. The image of Alphonse looking down at him was something he had grown strangely accustomed to throughout the course of his life, and this time seemed just like all the others.

"Hello, son," Alphonse said. "I'm glad to see you are awake."

"That makes two of us," Solomon said. "Is mom back?"

Alphonse smiled and nodded. "She was returned late last night. It was all because of you. You did it."

"We got him," Solomon said.

Alphonse handed him a copy of the day's newspaper. The headline read: "The Angelmaker Captured!" It showed a picture of Detective Hammett putting Serafino into a squad car.

"You got him," Alphonse said. "I have to say I am very impressed. With Serafino exposed to the world, none of his allies will risk helping him. Getting his picture in the paper was the final nail in his coffin."

"Taking him down was a small price to pay for Mom's safety," Solomon said. "Was she hurt when she got back?"

"Only her pride," Alphonse said. "She is a strong woman. She isn't used to someone else calling the shots. Not even me. She's resting now. Obviously, she was exhausted from the whole ordeal."

"And Milton?"

"A ghost like always," Alphonse said. "I'm not sure what will change as a result of all of this, but I think the balance of power has shifted in some way. The implications of Serafino's arrest probably won't be fully realized for quite some time."

"Then it sounds like my work here is done."

"Oh?"

"I'm ready to go home," Solomon said. "I need a week or two of vacation. What do I need to do to get out of this bed?"

"You're in pretty bad shape," Alphonse said. "Maybe it's best if you stay here for a day or two. Besides, this is home."

Solomon gave him a look. "Let's not do this right now. I'm not prepared to come back here to live. I've proven myself to be a completely capable and competent investigator. You've seen it with your own eyes. So, isn't it possible that being part of the family business isn't what's best for me? Maybe following my own path is best."

"Perhaps," Alphonse said. "Maybe we can revisit the discussion at another time. There's just one thing I want to say to you. It's long overdue."

"And what's that?"

"I'm a bad man," Alphonse admitted. "I know that. I'm a bad father. I know that as well. I've done a lot of things I regret. I can't go back and undo the damage I've caused. But I want to make amends. I mentioned this before you left the other day, and I'm mentioning it again now. I want to make things right between us."

Solomon studied his father's face, searching for signs of sincerity. Alphonse Sharpe was a cold, reptilian man who rarely showed any emotion, and this time was no different than any other. But his words were different, and that was something that Solomon wasn't used to. Alphonse was never penitent. When recruiting him to go after Serafino, Alphonse could have simply been apologetic as a means of getting Solomon to do his bidding. But what was the motive now? Solomon still didn't trust his father, but he couldn't come up with a good reason for the change of heart. He wasn't ready to say any of this was genuine just yet. He hated being so skeptical, but life had taught him to view things like this through a jaded lens.

"Let's take it day by day," Solomon said at last. "I'm not saying yes, but I'm not saying no either. If there is a path to reconciliation through all this then I am open to it. But I need time to process everything that has happened here."

Alphonse nodded. "I understand. Take all the time you need. I'll fetch Bertram."

CHAPTER 24

Bertram strongly advised Solomon not to leave his bed, but as always, Solomon was stubborn. He struggled out of the bed with the intent to head back to his apartment.

"I can rest at home just as easily as I can rest here," Solomon protested. "Help me get all of these tubes and electrodes off me."

"I don't advise any of this," Bertram said, exasperated. "You can rest at home, but you can't monitor your own health like I can. You also don't have access to the equipment and medicines we have here."

"Maybe not, but I'll risk it. I am going to take it easy for the next few days. I will take care of myself. Promise."

"Nothing I say will change your mind," Bertram sighed. "I am well aware of the hardheaded streak that runs through the Sharpe family. Will you at least take the meds if I send them with you?"

"Of course, Bertram," Solomon said. "I appreciate the help. I'm sure you saved my life."

"I did, indeed," the Sharpe family physician said. "You should also go to great lengths to avoid any fights for the foreseeable future. Your ribs are cracked in several places like dead branches."

"Believe me, I will avoid fighting at all costs. Every breath makes it feel like I've got broken glass in my lungs."

"That won't change for a while, I'm afraid. Make sure to ice the ribs liberally and take pain meds as needed. I made sure not to give you anything habit forming. Just some extra strength ibuprofen."

"I'll be good," Solomon said. "I promise. I'll do exactly as you say."

"That isn't completely true," Bertram said with a wry smile. "After all, you're preparing to walk out of here."

"Fair enough," Solomon said with a tired smile. "Can I ask you a question that has nothing to do with my health?"

"Fire away, sir," Bertram said. "I live to serve."

"Emily has been here for a few days. Has she been happy the entire time?"

Bertram seemed surprised by the question. "Well, yes sir," he replied. "I'm sensing your question has some deeper meaning that I'm not grasping and perhaps relates to the situation that brought about your current injuries. But you will need to be a bit clearer about what you want to know."

"I know you are loyal to my father, and I don't want to ask anything that would put you in a precarious situation with him. I just want to make sure she has been completely safe while she has been here."

"Why wouldn't she be, sir? She had every reason to be happy over the course of the last week. She's been here with her grandparents. They indulge her every whim. What child wouldn't be happy in that environment?"

Solomon went rigid at Bertram's answer. "You said she's been here with her grandparents?"

"That's right, sir. You seem troubled by the fact."

"Was my mother here the entire time?"

"Of course, sir. As far as I'm aware, she never left. Where

did you think she was?"

Solomon hurried over to the chair where his clothing had been neatly stacked. Someone had taken the liberty of washing everything he came in wearing. He quickly began to dress as his mind raced.

"What the devil is wrong with you?" Bertram asked.

"The devil is exactly what's wrong with me," Solomon said as he shimmied into his pants. "Do you happen to know where my mother is?"

"I believe she's tending to her orchids in the hothouse," Bertram said.

"Thank you again, Bertram. Sincerely."

"You're welcome, sir," Bertram said, fully aware that he had said something he shouldn't have said but unable to figure out what it was.

***

It was exactly as Bertram had said. Elise Sharpe was out in the greenhouse replanting some of her orchids. The air inside the glass structure was hot and stifling, and bees flew around liberally, looking for blossoms to pollinate. Solomon hated the greenhouse and he swatted at several of the bees that got too close to his head. He made no effort to mask his approach, storming in like he owned the place.

Calmly, his mother stood up and opened her arms to him, beckoning him near for a hug. "My poor Solomon," she said. "I'm so glad to see you up and about."

"Cut the crap," he said. "I know."

Elise Sharpe maintained her smile, but something about her

eyes changed. "What do you mean?"

"You were never kidnapped by anyone. You've been here the entire time."

Elise nodded calmly and put down the gardening tools she had been holding. "Maybe you are turning into a full-fledged investigator after all. I underestimated you."

"That seems to be everyone's opinion of me lately," Solomon said.

"You did a good thing last night," Elise said. "You helped bring a cold-blooded killer to justice."

"I think all I did was get one cold-blooded killer out of the way so two more cold-blooded killers could rise to power," Solomon said. "Isn't that right, Milton?"

Elise flashed her teeth in a smile that would have looked at home on the face of any bloodthirsty predator. "In Paradise Lost, Milton portrayed the Devil as a sympathetic figure. Milton viewed him through a rebellious prism and thought of him as a political revolutionary. It seems only fitting that people like your father and I adopt similar roles as we attempt to remake Valley Falls in our own image."

"To what end?" Solomon said, scarcely able to believe that his mother was wrapped up in something so Machiavellian.

"There is no end until the city is ours to do with as we please," she said. "The flame that is Valley Falls burns bright, and it's time we took hold of it."

"What has happened to you? Why all this secrecy to get me to do your bidding?"

"Your father was going to play the villain and hope you didn't find out about him. He thought using Emily was a stroke of brilliance. I thought it was risky. When you did learn of his involvement, we thought it only fitting to draw me into the deception as well. It raised the stakes and kept you in the game. As for why we went all cloak-and-dagger, it's because we had to. You wouldn't have cooperated any other way. The game demanded it."

"The game of eliminating all of the other players so the two of you win by default?"

"Exactly," Elise Sharpe said.

"And how do I know that the two of you aren't worse than the psycho we just knocked off the playing field?"

"You know because we raised you. No matter what you think of your father or me, you know that we aren't cold-blooded serial killers."

"If you had asked me a week ago, I would have said you definitely weren't serial killers. Now, I'm not sure of anything."

"We aren't that different from the people you thought you knew. We thrive on power and authority, but we also know that certain balances have to be maintained. We will make sure those balances remain."

"So, which one of you is the head of the organization and which one of you is the neck that turns it?" Solomon asked.

"It works in the faction as it works in life. Your father is the symbolic head, but he does my bidding. It's said behind every good man is a good woman. Let's just say, in this case, that behind every powerful man is an even more powerful woman."

"This is unbelievable," Solomon said. "My mother is an overlord."

"You make it sound so horrible," Elise Sharpe said. "I'm not as bad as you think I am."

"Aren't you?"

"I won't be able to convince you, so I won't even try."

"So what happens now?"

"What happens now is that you go back to your life, and to your P.I. business, and you move on with your life. You leave the secrets to us and lay your head down at night with the knowledge that the status quo in Valley Falls has been restored. Serafino Bartoli was leading our group in the wrong direction, and his tastes ran toward savagery and bloodlust. We will right the course of the ship now. Our tastes run more toward extravagance and wealth."

"Cruelty is commonly found in both bloodlust and wealth."

"You will just have to trust that we will behave ourselves."

"And if I decide not to slip back comfortably into my old life? What then? What if I decide to expose the two of you for what you really are?"

"Then you run the risk of allowing someone much worse than us to gain control of this city, and I promise you don't want that. There's also the small matter of what might happen to Emily, to Jenny, to Detective Hammett. We could make their lives very difficult. Yours too, if it came right down to it."

"Are you threatening your own family?" Solomon asked, scarcely believing he was hearing things correctly. "If that's the case, then maybe I judged you correctly the first time and am right to be wary of you."

"It's not even a subject to discuss," Elise said. "Just do as your mother tells you to and everything will work itself out. You have nothing to worry about."

"You want me to just pretend that none of this ever happened? You want me to forget everything I've learned over the past three days?"

"Not at all," Elise said. "You've proven yourself valuable to us. We will be using your services again. Sooner or later some situation will arise that will demand your specific set of skills, and we will call you. When that happens, we expect you to do whatever we ask because to do otherwise would allow the wolves to gather at the door. And we can't allow that."

"You want me to work for you?" Solomon said, laughing at the absurdity of such a thing.

"We demand it," Elise Sharpe said. "This, not hedge funds and money management, is the true family business. It's time you did your part."

"And I don't have any say in the matter?"

"Yes and no," Elise said. "You always have the right to refuse, but I wouldn't advise it. Cooperating with us will mean good things for all the people you care about. Jenny's life will improve in unexpected ways that she can't quite explain and certainly didn't expect. Emily's future will burn bright as every opportunity is laid out before her like a red carpet. Detective Hammett will be allowed to ride off into the sunset and retire in a blaze of glory. His book on the Angelmaker will be a guaranteed best-seller. Your business will explode and grow in ways you never dreamed, and your career will thrive, allowing you to experience some of the most basic creature comforts that life can provide…like food and reliable electricity."

"Sounds like a bribe," Solomon said.

Elise shook her head. "It's more of a down payment on the future."

"Isn't there anything you can say to make me feel good about your proposal?" Solomon asked.

Elise thought about this for a moment. "How about we

broker a deal of sorts?"

"I'm listening."

"We will only send you after criminals. So, no matter what our motives for involving you are, you can act with the knowledge that you've helped do something good for our fair city."

"That's a guarantee?" Solomon asked.

"Yes, I swear it. Any target we require you to take down will allow you to do so with a clean conscience because you know they deserve whatever comes to them."

"That's one step away from making me a vigilante."

"Maybe. But this is the closest we can get to making things legitimate."

"I guess it will have to do," Solomon said.

"So, it's a deal?"

"I don't really have the option to say no," Solomon sighed. "But I do have a few requests."

"Name them."

"I don't want to know what the two of you are into. Whatever it is, I'm probably better off not knowing."

"That sounds fair to me," Elise said. "Anything else?"

"Yes, I want your assurance that as long as I cooperate that those close to me are protected. That's not the same as an assurance that they won't be harmed. Jenny. Emily. Hammett. Peter Silverstone. They are guarded by your people. In the shadows, of course. No more killing."

"Fine," Elise said with a dismissive wave of the hand. "Are we done?"

"One more thing. I promised Angelo in exchange for his help that I would connect him with a patron to support his art. I want you to be that patron. Give him everything he needs to be successful."

"Very well. Now, will you go home and take care of yourself? You look like death warmed over."

"Yes," Solomon said. "And I'm taking Emily with me. I don't want her here for another second."

"Suit yourself," Elise Sharpe said.

EPILOGUE

If Solomon thought facing off against the Angelmaker was bad, facing off against Jenny was even worse once she found out that Emily had been with his parents the entire time. He was very careful about what information he revealed and what he kept to himself. No matter how much he wanted Jenny to know he was one of the good guys, he couldn't risk letting her know that Alphonse and Elise Sharpe were actually two of the not-good guys. He still wasn't entirely sure if the two of them could be classified as bad per se, but he was absolutely sure that they weren't completely on the side of good.

Things were tense with Jenny for the next few weeks, but eventually she thawed a little bit where he was concerned. Based on what she had gone through, he couldn't blame her for being upset with him, but he also couldn't tell her why she shouldn't be upset with him. All he could do was hope that time would heal all wounds.

Meanwhile, his relationship with Emily grew better and stronger than ever. After feeling like he had nearly lost her, he resolved not to take his time with her for granted. Instead, he focused more on being the father and friend she deserved. She was oblivious to the reasons behind Solomon's newfound attention, but like any young girl who loves her father, she was happy for any time they spent together.

The case against Serafino Bertoli was fast and severe. Detective Hammett practically handed the case to the D.A. on a silver platter. Within six weeks, Bertoli was tried for the murders of the five Angelmaker victims, found guilty on all counts, and sentenced to life in prison. The speed with which the trial took place was nearly unprecedented. If such things weren't viewed as ludicrous, you might have thought that someone was pulling the strings behind the scenes to make sure justice was served swiftly…

But, of course, that was the kind of thinking best reserved for the paranoid and those who dabbled in conspiracy theory.

For his part in the Angelmaker investigation, Detective Hammett became an overnight sensation, appearing on a variety of television programs, giving a host of news interviews, and telling his story through a series of magazine articles. The media loved him and made him a celebrity within a matter of weeks. He announced his retirement from the force not long after selling the book rights to his story about the Angelmaker case.

In other news, without the influence of his father being used to keep him locked away in Saturn Hills Asylum, Angelo Bertoli was finally free again, and he went about the business of trying to piece his life together after having the past year stolen from him. Although he didn't really need therapy during the time he was incarcerated in the asylum, he found that he definitely needed it afterward. He continued to see Dr. Norman Blackthorn in the weeks that followed, and he spent most of his time talking about how his visions of angels had gotten more and more severe and intense. There were times where some of the things he said almost seemed possible. But, gradually, after he was sponsored by an anonymous patron who claimed to be a fan of his painting, Angelo dug his way out of the dark pit of guilt and remorse and found some success in the local art circuit.

Peter Silverstone recovered quite nicely from his gunshot wound and was galvanized by the experience at the Lamplight Theatre. Having seen for himself that he had the skills necessary to be a world class illusionist like his father, Silverstone began work on an act that would put the family name on the lips of everyone again.

Like most things in life, the vividness of the Angelmaker mystery eventually faded for Solomon, as did his connection to the main players in the case. Solomon did his very best to return to a normal life and put all of the events of the ordeal behind him. He tried to forget about the things he knew, and gradually, after recovering from his injuries and getting back to work, the day-to-day grind of case work gave him something else to concentrate on.

With his life back on track, Solomon was mostly successful in forgetting about that last conversation he had with his mother and the implications of what it all might mean.

Then, one fateful night, about six months after the conclusion of the Angelmaker case, something happened that brought all of the old fears and worries crashing down around him.

Solomon came home after a particularly hard day of investigating and saw a red envelope sitting on his kitchen table. His breath caught in his throat, and his heart triphammered in his chest as he pulled out a familiar-looking card bearing the image of a devil on one side.

The text that was written on the other side was simple and to the point:

"Solomon, it's time to take a job for us. We will provide

details soon…"

Solomon started to tear the card up and throw it in the trash can. But he knew it wouldn't do any good. One way or another he would end up involved. Until then, all he could do was do his best to relax and enjoy his life. It was scarce consolation for the bloody days that were sure to lie up ahead. But it would have to do.

The End

***

About the Author

Jason Brannon is the author of *The Tears of Nero*, *The Cage*, and many other novels and short story collections. He is also the co-creator of The Deadbolt Mystery Society. His work has been translated into German and optioned for film. He loves horror movies, Sherlock Holmes stories, video games, rock music and escape rooms. While he knows all there is to know about the town of Valley Falls mentioned in this book, he would never live there.

www.ingramcontent.com/pod-product-compliance
Ingram Content Group UK Ltd.
Pitfield, Milton Keynes, MK11 3LW, UK
UKHW022022190726
13853UKWH00005B/2067

9 798521 769513